Date Due

AMERICAN HUMORISTS SERIES

BAWLFREDONIA

by   Jonas Clopper

LITERATURE HOUSE / GREGG PRESS
Upper Saddle River, N. J.

Republished in 1969 by
LITERATURE HOUSE
an imprint of The Gregg Press
121 Pleasant Avenue
Upper Saddle River, N. J. 07458

Standard Book Number—8398-0268-4
Library of Congress Card—79-91076

Printed in United States of America

THE AMERICAN HUMORISTS

Art Buchwald, Bob Hope, Red Skelton, S. J. Perelman, and their like may serve as reminders that the "cheerful irreverence" which W. D. Howells, two generations ago, noted as a dominant characteristic of the American people has not been smothered in the passage of time. In 1960 a prominent Russian literary journal called our comic books "an infectious disease." Both in Russia and at home, Mark Twain is still the best-loved American writer; and Mickey Mouse continues to be adored in areas as remote as the hinterland of Taiwan. But there was a time when the mirthmakers of the United States were a more important element in the gross national product of entertainment than they are today. In 1888, the British critic Grant Allen gravely informed the readers of the *Fortnightly*: "Embryo Mark Twains grow in Illinois on every bush, and the raw material of *Innocents Abroad* resounds nightly, like the voice of the derringer, through every saloon in Iowa and Montana." And a half-century earlier the English reviewers of our books of humor had confidently asserted them to be "the one distinctly original product of the American mind"—"an indigenous home growth." Scholars are today in agreement that humor was one of the first vital forces in making American literature an original entity rather than a colonial adjunct of European culture.

The American Humorists Series represents an effort to display both the intrinsic qualities of the national heritage of native prose humor and the course of its development. The books are facsimile reproductions of original editions hard to come by—some of them expensive collector's items. The series includes examples of the early infiltration of the autochthonous into the stream of jocosity and satire inherited from Europe but concentrates on representative products of the outstanding practitioners. Of these the earliest in point of time are the exemplars of the Yankee "Down East" school, which began to flourish in the 1830's—and, later, provided the cartoonist Thomas Nast with the idea for Uncle Sam, the national personality in striped pants. The series follows with the chief humorists who first used the Old Southwest as setting. They were the founders of the so-called frontier humor.

The remarkable burgeoning of the genre during the Civil War period is well illustrated in the books by David R. Locke, "Bill Arp," and others who accompanied Mark Twain on the way to fame in the jesters' bandwagon. There is a volume devoted to Abraham Lincoln as jokesmith and spinner of tall tales. The wits and satirists of the Gilded Age, the Gay Nineties, and the first years of the present century round out the sequence. Included also are several works which mark the rise of Negro humor, the sort that made the minstrel show the first original contribution of the United States to the world's show business.

The value of the series to library collections in the field of American literature is obvious. And since the subjects treated in these books, often with surprising realism, are intimately involved with the political and social scene, and the Civil War, and above all possess sectional characteristics, the series is also of immense value to the historian. Moreover, quite a few of the volumes carry illustrations by the ablest cartoonists of their day, a matter of interest to the student of the graphic arts. And, finally, it should not be overlooked that the specimens of Negro humor offer more tangible evidence of the fixed stereotyping of the Afro-American mentality than do the slave narratives or the abolitionist and sociological treatises.

The American Humorists Series shows clearly that a hundred years ago the jesters had pretty well settled upon the topics that their countrymen were going to laugh at in the future—from the Washington merry-go-round to the pranks of local hillbillies. And as for the tactics of provoking the laugh, these old masters long since have demonstrated the art of titillating the risibilities. There is at times mirth of the high-brow variety in their pages: neat repartee, literary parody, Attic salt, and devastating irony. High seriousness of purpose often underlies their fun, for many of them wrote with the conviction that a column of humor was more effective than a page of editorials in bringing about reform or combating entrenched prejudices. All of the time-honored devices of the lowbrow comedians also abound: not only the sober-faced exaggeration of the tall tale, outrageous punning, and grotesque spelling, but a boisterous Homeric joy in the rough-and-tumble. There may be more beneath the surface, however, for as one of their number, J. K. Bangs, once remarked, these old humorists developed "the exuberance of feeling and a resentment of restraint that have helped to make us the free and independent people that we are." The native humor is indubitably American, for it is infused with the customs, associations, convictions, and tastes of the American people.

PROFESSOR CLARENCE GOHDES
Duke University
January, 1969 *Durham, North Carolina*

Jonas Clopper, a minister of Baltimore, Maryland, wrote one of the most curious political parables in the history of the genre. *Fragments of the History of Bawlfredonia*, which appeared in 1819, is indebted to *Gulliver's Travels*, to books of travel and exploration, and to the mass of polemical literature that appeared after the American Revolution. This sort of writing increased in bitterness when the new Republic defeated England in the War of 1812 and began to show a marked lack of reverence for the forms and customs of her former rulers. Clopper omits very little in his list of vices to be castigated, and freely identifies anything democratic with anarchy and depravity. The major attack of his satiric allegory is directed against Thomas Jefferson. Paine, Madison, and Franklin are secondary targets. Jefferson is described as a coward who, although possessing a numerically superior force, retreated during the Revolution. Clopper also levels the more damaging accusation that Jefferson had relations with various slave women. This sort of slander was quite popular in the first half of the nineteenth century—William W. Brown's *Clotel, or The President's Daughter* is a full-length novel based on "miscegenation in high places" nonsense. Clopper's Jefferson, who rules the land of "Blackmoreland," is also represented as a heathen and a Frenchified atheist (one is never sure which) who doesn't care whether a man worships one God or fifty, as long as his black Venus is not taken from him. Clopper proceeds from scurrilous attacks on Jefferson's character to declamations against Deism, laboratory science, and the doctrine of the perfectibility of man. Jeffersonians are accused, among other things, of maintaining that men were originally tadpoles.

After some fulsome comments on various politicians, Clopper attempts to summarize the characters of Yankees and Southerners. Oddly enough, his grotesque, pop-art caricatures, exaggerated and fulminating with malice, delineate rather accurately the salient traits of both of these nearly extinct species: [Yankees are] "a sober, ploding [*sic*], industrious, saving, and economic race. They would rarely open their minds fully and plainly to any one; yet they were extremely inquisitive." In true pulpit style, Clopper assails the weaknesses of the Southern planter-aristocrats—"Eating, drinking, and wenching. . ."—but fails to note, or refuses to acknowledge, their finer qualities of chivalry, hospitality, and generosity.

Clopper's most amusing diatribe is reserved for the "stinkum-puff" of Virginia, the foul weed of the following origin: At the beginning of the world, a mysterious woman appeared from the sky, seated herself on the ground, and then fled. "Where her right hand rested, they found corn; where her left rested, pulse (lentils); and, precisely under her posteriors, they found STINKUM-PUFF."

It is unlikely that Clopper would welcome the idea of seeing his satire included in a series of "American Humorists," but it is only with amusement that one can read his furious anti-democratic outbursts, his obsession with the mixing of the races, and his narrow, Calvinistic distrust of human nature.

It should be a delight for the scholar to visit the now-deserted battlefields where conflicting ideas, once of vital importance to civilization, struggled for supremacy. Fortunately for civilization (and pipe smokers), the demons and fiends of democracy and pleasure which dwelt in Bawlfredonia triumphed before the end of the century, and, with the exception of intermarriage, are now respectable citizens.

Upper Saddle River, N. J.   F. C. S.
May, 1969

FRAGMENTS

OF THE HISTORY

OF

BAWLFREDONIA:

CONTAINING

AN ACCOUNT OF THE DISCOVERY AND SETTLEMENT,

OF

THAT GREAT SOUTHERN CONTINENT;

AND OF THE FORMATION AND PROGRESS OF THE

Bawlfredonian Commonwealth.

BY HERMAN THWACKIUS.

TRANSLATED FROM THE ORIGINAL BAWLFREDONIAN MANUSCRIPT, INTO THE
FRENCH LANGUAGE, BY MONSIEUR TRADUCTEUR, AND RENDERED INTO EN-
GLISH, BY A CITIZEN OF AMERICA

PRINTED FOR THE

AMERICAN BOOKSELLERS.

1819.

DISTRICT OF MARYLAND—To wit.

BE IT REMEMBERED, That on the twenty-first day of July, in the forty-fourth year of the Independence of the United States of America, Jonas Clopper, of the said district, hath deposited in this office, the title of a book, the right whereof he claims as author, in the words following to wit:—

L. S.

"Fragments of the History of Bawlfredonia: containing an account of the discovery and settlement, of that great Southern Continent; and of the formation and progress of the Bawlfredonian Commonwealth; By Herman Thwackihs. Translated from the original Bawlfredonian manuscript, into the French language, by Monsieur Traducteur, and rendered into English, by a citizen of America."

In conformity to an act of the Congress of the United States, entitled "An act for the encouragement of learning, by securing the copies of maps, charts, and books, to the authors and proprietors of such copies during the times therein mentioned;" and also to the act, entitled "An act supplementary to the act, entitled 'An act for the encouragement of learning, by securing the copies of maps, charts, and books to the authors and proprietors of such copies, during the times therein mentioned;' and extending the benefits thereof to the arts of designing, engraving, and etching, historical and other prints."

PHILIP MOORE,
Clerk of the District of Maryland

DEDICATIO.

CELEBERRIMO SAMUELI ELL CENTUMVIRO, M. D.
—L. L. D. Antiquario, &c. &c. &c. maxime illuminati
regni super hunc orbem mundanum,—patrono et defenso-
ri et interpreti omnium avium, ossium, animalium, plan-
tarum, concharum et piscium, quæ hic gignuntur, vel has
in oras, migrant, ab áêre, ab oceanis, vel maribus, vel
insulis, vel continentibus, mittit salutem.—*Translator*.

Item. Serenissime, maxime magnanime, valde eru-
dite et dignissime reipublicæ literarum præses—tibi ab
imo corde, hæc fragmenta, Bawlfredoniæ historiæ in-
scripsi. Fama vestra, dignitas centum societates sustin-
ens, gloria et nomen vestrum, clarissime diffusum inter
gentes terrarum orbis, instar clypeí sextemplicis, ab om-
nibus, irruptionibus, et impetibus hostilibus has chartas
defendent.

Sapientia vestrâ perspicietur me aliquas reliquias pre-
ciosissimas arcanorum gentis remotissimæ, et valde an-
tiquæ, cujus leges, instituta, mores sunt aliena ab omni-
bus populis, multo sudoris, assecutum esse. Tibi bene
notam suspicor hanc rempublicam Bawlfredoniæ.

Horum Fragmentorum scriptor, de regibus, impera-
toribus, consulibus, proconsulibus, demonibus, et multis
aliis rebus sublimibus, verbis grande sonantibus, cicinit,
ut spero hac in mea versione sublucet, quam sub pedibus
vestris deposui.

Denique, laudes tuas ad astra sustuli hac in inscrip-
tione, cummaxima spe legis talionis.

TRANSLATOR.

FRAGMENTS

OF THE

HISTORY OF BAWLFREDONIA.

Introduction.

THE celebrated Mr. Addison has enumerated *novelty* amongst the sources of the pleasures of imagination. All writers on the subjects of taste and criticism, since his time, have given their suffrage to his speculations. An author who ventures his lucubrations before the publick, must remember that in order to gain the favour of that publick, there must be, at least, something novel in his work:—the more the better. I, therefore, take it for granted, that if I can exhibit a work consisting altogether of novelties, facts wholly unknown to the civilized world even to this moment, I shall be pretty certain of no ordinary share of attention as an American writer.

By a most novel coincidence of circumstances, I think this completely in my power. I shall, indeed, be no more than a translator of a translation. But as the original and the translation are both in manu-

B

script, and as there never was, to my knowledge, any more than one copy of each, I have the merit, as to the world, and the pleasure derived from the following work, of an entire original, and I hope to be rewarded with a proportional degree of applause. As to the novelty of the relations which are contained in this work, I feel confident there can be no doubt.

As the strangeness of the facts, as well as their novelty, may excite doubts in the minds of incredulous people as to their reality, I shall proceed to give a circumstantial account of the manner in which I became possessed of them.

It is well known that in the year 1785, De La Perouse, a French navigator, of great celebrity, set sail from Brest on a voyage of discovery The extent of his researches were to be bounded only by the globe itself. The mighty Atlantick and Pacifick oceans were to disclose to him the innumerable treasures contained in their bosoms, while the shores of the old and new worlds were to enrich his journals with their various curiosities and wonders. In 1786, he reached the eastern coast of South America, around which he coasted until he arrived at Connection Bay on the west, about 44 deg. south latitude. Here he made some stay, and having recruited his stores, and the health of his crew, he set sail across the vast Pacifick; and, after touching at innumerable islands, he arrived safe at Bherring's Bay, coasted down the western coast of North America until he reached the Bay of St. Anthony. Thence he stretched his course across the Pacifick; and, after visiting the numerous islands and groups of islands, in that world of waters, and performing a voyage of more than twelve thousand miles, he arrived at Canton in China. Making but a short stay in that mart of European commerce, he visited the Philippine islands. He then steered northward, coasting the eastern coast of Asia, until he arrived at Kamtschatka in the year 1787. He again changed his course, explored the Pacifick ocean from those northerly regions, where mountains of ice float on the bosom of the sea to Botany Bay in the eastern coast of New Holland, about 34 deg. south latitude.

At this receptacle of the filth and wretchedness of the British empire, our unfortunate navigator arrived near the latter end of the year 1787, more than two years after his embarkation at Brest.

On the 4th of January following, he set sail from Botany Bay, and never was heard of afterwards, until the novel manuscript from which the following pages are translated, give some further account of him.

He explored New Holland, and Vandieman's Land; and about one year after he had departed from Botany Bay, arrived at Asylum Harbour, on the coast of New Holland, to the northward of Vandieman's Land, a part of that great southern continent, as it may justly be denominated, which had never before been visited by any European navigator. He ran into the harbour before a *father of a breeze*, to which every sail was spread. His soundings indicated a good bottom, and deep water near the shore.

The mildness of the weather, the deep and luxuriant forests, the exquisite beauty and grandeur of the mountains, which stretched across and skirted the horizon to the northeast, between Asylum Harbour and Botany Bay, and the appearance of cultivated fields and of houses, tempted Monsieur Traducteur, a young gentleman of handsome literary accomplishments, who had accompanied De La Perouse on his voyage, to go on shore with the first boat sent off to explore the land.

They had scarcely touched the strand when a storm arose. The wind blew from the land with the most appalling fury. The boat was rent from her moorings. But what filled the hearts of Monsieur Traducteur and his little party with the utmost horror, was, that the ship which had carried themselves, their brave captain, and fellow sailors over every sea, was torn from her anchors by the rage of the tempest, and hurried before the roaring storm and angry billows before their sight. Torrents of rain poured from the clouds, accompanied with loud peals of thunder, Monsieur Traducteur and his companions fled for shelter to some neighbouring rocks, which, jutting over the sandy beach, formed a covert for their protection.

In this wretched retreat Monsieur Traducteur and his companions spent a sleepless night, whilst the storm roared around them, and the waves broke at their feet. At the approach of the dawn, the tempest ceased, the clouds passed away, and the morning sun rose on a tranquil scene, some remaining billows gently rolled towards the shore, and went to sleep on the strand. But no boat or ship was seen, and De La Perouse was never more heard of.

Most desolate was the situation of Monsieur Traducteur and his companions, without food or any other necessaries, save the clothing which they wore, upon an unknown island, uncertain what reception they were to meet with from the natives, and totally destitute of the means of defence or retreat.

The young gentleman however was pious. He raised his hands to heaven in the midst of his dispirited companions in misfortune, and commended himself to the protection of a gracious providence, through that redeemer in whom he trusted. They then left their retreat.

Upon ascending the rocks and travelling a short distance into the country, how great was their astonishment to find fields that indicated a high state of cultivation, and habitations, in which dwelt people, neatly though strangely dressed, of fair complexion, in whose faces there were expressions of intelligence, benevolence, and dignity.

They instantly perceived that these people, though plain in their manners, could not be savages. Every face bore great marks of civilization. Even in China, Monsieur Traducteur had witnessed nothing equal to these people. He and the sailors were received with the greatest hospitality. Though he did not understand a single word of their language, and all their intercourse was at first carried on by signs, yet he soon formed an uncommon attachment to these strangers. He immediately applied himself to the study of their language, which he found to be copious. Great facilities were afforded him; for every body seemed to be extremely talkative. As soon as he was able to understand their questions, a prodigious multitude of interrogatories were poured in upon him from every quarter. Men, women, and children, of all ranks and conditions, annoyed him with inquiries Their good nature however, hospitality. and the progress which he daily made in the acquisition of their tongue, made most ample amends for the little uneasiness occasioned by this curiosity. In fine, he soon found that he was thrown by providence amongst an enlightened and Christian, though somewhat rude people, who formed a great empire, called the republick of Bawlfredonia. His brother tars mingled with the multitude, learned their language, married their daughters, and soon became prominent, and important members of their commonwealth. Monsieur Traducteur's patron and preceptor in the Bawlfredonian language, had possession of a large library, containing many curious manuscripts on a great variety of subjects. Amongst other objects of great interest, which attracted the attention of Monsieur Traducteur, he discovered a manuscript, or rather a number of manuscripts, containing a history of the discovery, settlement, and progress of the commonwealth of Bawlfredonia.

As soon as he became sufficiently acquainted with the Bawlfredonian language he commenced a translation of the work into French. Various notes were added by the translator in his progress, which tend greatly to illustrate the history and condition of that wonderful people.

Losing all hopes of ever returning to his native land, he allied himself by marriage to the family of Augustus Thwackius, esq. the great grandson of the immortal Herman Thwackius, author of the History of Bawlfredonia, with which I am about to favour the publick.

Monsieur Traducteur being a man of an inquisitive and enterprising genius, was thought to be a fit person to conduct a governmental expedition, for the purpose of exploring the central regions of Bawlfredonia, which lay to the north of the great mountains mentioned above.

Though upwards of forty five years of age, and enjoying ease and affluence, he accepted of the appointment, and set out on his tour of exploration, in the autumn of the year eighteen hundred and twelve. After having passed the great mountains, he found a most charming champaign country, inhabited by various races of savage tribes. He at length arrived at a large river, where he found a boat navigated by white men who appeared to be civilized. In this boat he found an accomplished Irish gentleman, who spoke the French language fluently. This gentleman was my friend Cowan Callaghan, esq. who, fourteen years before that time, had been banished to Botany Bay for writing a political pamphlet, in which he had the hardihood to assert "that Ireland was held by conquest, that the majority of the Irish had never given their consent to the government by which they were held in durance, and that of course, England possessed no lawful authority to govern "that sweet little isle of the ocean."

To find such a man was a very joyful event to Monsieur Traducteur. Although he had spoken little French for the last twenty-four years of his life, they did not fail to *parlez vous* with wonderful volubility, for which both nations are sufficiently remarkable.

Our gentleman from Bawlfredonia had carried with him a copy of his translation of the celebrated Thwackius's history. It was of course shewn to the exiled Hibernian, who was perfectly enraptured with it, and prevailed upon Traducteur to bestow it upon him for the use of the civilized world in the northern hemisphere.

The Frenchman did not part with his papers without great reluctance. As the Bawlfredonian manuscript, however, still existed, to which he could have access, and as he was willing the world should hear of his adopted country, of himself, and his exploits, and above all, as the openness, candour, and warm heart of the Irishman had captivated him, he marked the circumstances relative to his story on the envelope of the packet, and put the treasure into the hands of 'Squire Callaghan. I need not add that they parted with many protestations of everlasting friendship, though they should never meet again. Monsieur Traducteur pursued the object of his expedition to enrich his, and his king's cabinet with spe-

C

cimens and descriptions of the profuse wealth, beauty and grandeur of this great southern continent, resolving not to forsake the country and the friends who had generously adopted and enriched him. Mr. Callaghan hastened back to Botany Bay, elated with his literary treasure, and hoping to immortalize himself, by giving to Europe, a knowledge of a new and marvellous empire. He even thought his fourteen years' exile well rewarded by the kindness of providence, who had thrown in his way the learned, polite, and generous Frenchman. Let us figure to ourselves what would be the cogitations of the exile while his bark gently glitted down the surface of a smooth stream, flowing through a shady grove in the stillness of the twilight, while the stars were just peeping through the mantle of the heavens. His term of exile was just then expired, and the first vessel, from Botany Bay for Europe, would convey him to his long unseen friends, fraught with vast information, collected by his own researches in regions almost unknown to Europe; and then, the immortal work of Thwackius. He must be celebrated wheresoever "*the violent Aufidus roars;*" the world must be filled 'ere long with his fame. But alas! how visionary and uncertain are all hopes of human grandeur! The vessel which conveyed 'Squire Callaghan in sight of Dublin was captured by an Ameri-

can privateer and brought into Baltimore, in the second year of the late glorious war with England.
Worthy Mr. Callaghan! you shall not be utterly
disappointed. Your name shall be handed down in
this work. You will have ample justice done to
your memory and your exertions. To your warm
heart which won the soul of the Frenchman, America and Europe is, or soon will be, indebted for the
pleasure and instruction which the two hemispheres
will derive from the pages of Thwackius—the immortal Thwackius!

It is unnecessary to state the manner in which the
manuscript fell into my hands. In translating it into
the English language, I think I may, without vanity,
assert that I have done full justice to the original.

I should not have troubled either the reader, or
myself, with such a circumstantial account of the
events by which this work was brought into our highly favoured country, but that I might remove all
doubts relative to the authenticity of the history and
the truth of the facts which it contains. This became in some measure necessary, as they are of so
uncommon a nature, the national events, and the characters introduced, are so unlike any thing witnessed
in this country, and I may add in Europe, that I fear
many Americans will have doubts that the whole is
a fiction. I do assure them that the history of

Thwackius is as genuine, and the facts which it records as true, as that a great, valiant, and pious president of these United States, has ably conducted our late glorious war with England to a most honourable conclusion, and for ever secured "free trade and sailors' rights."

I am aware that there are some acute people, who can discover similarity between the events which befal nations and individuals, the most distant and dissimilar. These people may possibly fancy a resemblance between some of the characters and events of Bawlfredonia and this country. They may suspect, especially if they are ill-natured folks, that some satire is meant upon the great people of this "the most enlightened" commonwealth. I most sincerely entreat the reader not to suffer such evil suggestions to intrude themselves upon his brain. How is the thing possible? The Bawlfredonians never having been heard of before, how should they ever have heard of the United States of North America? Monsieur Traducteur may be suspected of making some ill-natured side remarks at this nation. Here again it must be remarked, that as he has been twenty five years, or thereabouts, in Bawlfredonia, in which time he has had no communication with any European, except the sailors who accompanied him on shore, and the Irishman, it is utterly impossible he should allude to any events which have taken place in these late years. But there is one consideration which must satisfy the most sceptical reader, that is, the immaculate purity of the characters, the transcendent intellectual powers which all our great men have possessed, both for civil and martial government, and the unparalleled prosperity to which they have, especially of late years, raised this flourishing commonwealth; all these, I say, set them far above the loftiest flights of the shafts of satire. Even the immortal Thwackius, who was certainly something of a satirist, were he now living and writing at this very desk, would not presume to aim an arrow at them.

As to the style and arrangement of the historical fragments in question, I must be indulged in a few remarks.

Translated into French, and then into English, the phraseology must be both modernised and *westernised*, in a great degree. As Dugal Stcuart, the celebrated metaphysician, says of some translations which he makes from the French of D'Alembert. "There may be some departures from the purity of English diction, but I was unwilling to impair the force of the original by making it perfect English." Though, like the aforesaid translator of the great man alluded to, nobody but myself may be able to discover the Gallicisms in which I shall occasionally indulge.

There may also be some flights of fancy, partaking of the *ore rotundo*, the *magniloquent* style of the ancients. These it seems, both the translator of the original manuscript and myself have thought proper to preserve, in order to retain, as far as consistent with our own tastes, the times and character of Thwackius, which are exhibited on his pages: and this especially, when very great men were the subject of remark. For example, when an immortal and heroick king, claps spurs to his steed in full view of the enemy, and thunders over the plain, flying from the presence of the foe, in sight of two hostile armies arrayed in dread battalia, and in sight of the vast metropolis of a huge empire, at the noise of the prancing of whose steed, "*Quadrupedante putrem sonnitie qualet ungula campum,*" the frogs plunge into their pools with tremendous splash, as they did long ago upon an occasion somewhat similar, when Jupiter sent them king Log, and dived to the bottom, alarmed at the presence of the flying monarch. Who, on such awfully sublime occasion, could avoid ascending to the very summit of Pindarick grandeur!

As to the arrangement of the work, and the degree of perfection given to it, criticism must be silent. I might plead, as is plead in behalf of Virgil's

Eneid, that the author never put a finishing hand to it; which is literally true. But such an apology is not necessary, for in fact we have only fragments, which the translator arranged and numbered according to the best light he could have. Hence it cannot, consistently with justice, be tried by the rules for historical composition, which have been laid down by our rhetoricians. However, I am decidedly of opinion, that it possesses one great advantage over those histories that carry on an unbroken narration from the rise to the downfal of a nation. In such histories, many pages and great labour to the reader and the writer are expended in recording events, which are of no importance at all to posterity. Not so these Thwackean fragments. They must be supposed to embrace the most important periods of the history of Bawlfredonia, passing over those epochs in which there were few events to court the attention of the historical muse. After all, many curious particulars are no doubt fallen into the gulf of oblivion, which devours both the great and the small. But here is Thwackius. Let him speak for himself.

HISTORICAL SKETCHES

OF THE

DISCOVERY OF BAWLFREDONIA,

AND OF ITS SETTLEMENT,

And the formation and progress of the Bawlfredonian Commonwealth.

The epoch of the discovery of Bawlfredonia is not fixed with precision by antiquarians. It was, however, many centuries ago. I shall proceed to relate a few of the most remarkable incidents attending that discovery, at the same time avoiding that prolixity of detail, into which too many of our historians have fallen.*

A celebrated navigator, Augustus Fredonius, of Hindostan, from the most careful observation, concluded that there must be a continent in the south. "For," said he, "it would be most unreasonable to suppose that there should be so much land on the north side, where the sun never shines perpendicu-

---

* Ned Neverout in giving the history of the three first years of his father's settlement in Bawlfredonia, consisting of thirty-three pages, actually wrote, by way of introduction, four hundred and fifty-five, giving an account of the discovery of the country —*Thwackius.*

D

larly, and none but small islands to the south." He solicited many of the petty nabobs to supply him with a vessel, even of the smallest size, and a sufficient number of seamen to navigate it, promising that he would discover a new continent, and lay it at the feet of his patron.

Though these nabobs were celebrated among their subjects, or rather their favourites, as persons of the most profound wisdom, nothing was more untrue. They were, in fact, a set of barbarous and ignorant asses, bred up in luxury and idleness, who would rather see a bull flayed alive by an expert butcher, than view the most brilliant display of art or nature. They not only rejected every proposition of Fredonius, but some of them were even so rude and fractious as to kick him out of doors as an impudent visionary.

Their slaves and toad-eaters approved of this conduct as much as Nestor did Agamemnon for beating the poor and unfortunate Thersites.*

Happily, great men are not easily discouraged. He bore with the insult of titled fools, in the cheering hope of accomplishing his favourite project. At length a princess of Seringapatam, queen Magnificenza, offered to go to the extent of her limited reve-

---

* How Thwackius became acquainted with this incident from Homer, antiquarians must decide.

nues in providing him a suitable naval equipment.
Two ships were soon got in readiness, one with
three and the other with two banks of oars, and the
most expert rowers in all Hindostan collected to man
them. A large stock of sea-stores was put on board.
On the day that commodore Fredonius embarked,
the queen, with all her friends, and many thousands
of the gaping multitude collected about the harbour to
shout success to the adventurous mariners. Many
prayers for their success were offered up by the
queen, who, as is commonly the case, was pious as
well as great.

A gentle breeze blew towards the south-east,
and filled the swelling sails, while the rowers kept
time, with the strokes of their oars, to grand and
martial musick, which was played upon instruments
peculiar to that country, and from which our Hypo-
sopnia is derived The admiral thought all this too
pompous, but submitted to it in order to gratify the
multitude, and to permit the rowers to shew their
dexterity before the princess Magnificenza. He
stood on the prow of the largest vessel, where his
flag waved in splendid majesty, with composed and
solemn aspect, revolving in his mighty mind the great
events which awaited his little squadron, and fondly
cherishing the hopes of earthly immortality. He, at
the same time, sent up devout prayers to heaven to

protect him, and enable him to explore the regions, and discover the great continent which he believed the creator had planted in the midst of the southern seas. As the group sunk from his sight, he waved his white handkerchief as a token of respectful and affectionate adieu to the princess.

And now gentle reader where do you imagine her royal husband, whom I scorn to name, was at this moment. No where else than in a filthy grog-shop, pouring out curses upon his wife, for what he was pleased to call her foolish prodigality. His slaves and toad-eaters were around him, exclaiming "Well said, your majesty."

But let us pursue the fleet. The admiral steered to the south, along the Corromandel coast, and then from island to island, until he arrived in sight of Bawlfredonia, after having been out more than eighteen months, and having lost many of his best men through fatigue and peril. Several storms had been encountered, the ships were somewhat crazy, and the remnant of his crew were sunk in despondency, when, like a stroke of electricity, they were roused by the cry of "Land!"

The figure of the land, the distant and lofty mountains, all seemed to indicate a great continent. The courses also, and complexion of the winds and tides, uniting with the theory of commodore Fredo-

nius, all tended to convince him, that the country before him would realize the utmost extent of his ex-
pectations.

Before he could reach the land, the threatening
clouds began to collect, the sun disappeared. A hollow roar of tremendous omen was heard through the
whole ethereal regions. The sea assumed a dark
and frightful hue. The billows were heaving under
the pressure of the rising winds. Dark fragments of
clouds seemed to sink down to salute the swelling
waves. From these fragments the lightnings flamed
along the sides of watery mountains, and appeared
to be extinguished among the breaking billows.
The loudest peals of thunder mingled their voices
with the roar of the tempest.

The land vanished from the sight of the affright-
ed mariners. They were driven with the velocity
of an arrow, they knew not whither. So dark was
the tempest, they scarcely distinguished when night
came. By the lashing of the waves their oars were
torn from the sides of their ships. All but the commodore gave themselves up for lost. Their time
was divided between prayers to heaven, and impre-
cations upon the head of Fredonius. Standing on
deck, lashed to the mast, he raised his eyes, his
hands, his voice and heart to heaven; and, in the pious fervour of devotion, thus addressed the Almighty

God, in whom he put his trust. "Thou Almighty Being, who rulest the vast universe, the winds and tempests are thy ministers; thou sendest them forth from the openings of thine hand. Allay the tempest, and save, we beseech thee, these thy poor servants: cast us not away in these unknown regions. We implore salvation from the fury of the raging deep for thy mercies' sake."* As soon as he had uttered this prayer, he ordered his men to their stations, saying, "I perceive some presages of an approaching calm, and without some dreadful accident, beyond any thing we have hitherto witnessed, our vessel will ride in safety through the storm for some hours more." Noble and devout man! your prospects were soon realized. The winds were soon hushed, the rain ceased to pour down from the heavens, the voice of the thunder was heard only at a distance, and soon the stars began to peep through the misty air.

Utterly ignorant as to the course in which the tempest had driven them, all stood in silent anxiety,

---

* I approve most heartily of this prayer recorded by our historian. Some *devout* men have blamed Virgil for making his hero pray too much. But, for myself, I think the prayers of Eneas more sublime than any other part of the Æneid. And although a late voyager has, in the opinion of a large portion of the *wise* men of his country, greatly marred his reputation as a philosophical historian, by recording his prayer on an occasion somewhat similar, yet I cannot, on that account, agree to omit this evidence of the piety of the immortal Fredonius.—*Am. Trans.*

waiting for the approach of day. The fate of their companions, in the other ship, was one of their greatest sources of solicitude, as they had been separated from them early in the storm. Before the approach of day they saw a light, which they hoped was the other vessel. At the dawn they were agreeably surprised on finding themselves near the opening of an extensive bay, into a most delightful country. The light they had discovered was from the shore. But the other ship was within less than one mile of them to the south-east; the harbour lay to the northeast.

I might stop to inquire whether it would be unphilosophical to attribute the assuaging of the tempest, and the salvation of these mariners, to an immediate interposition of heaven, in answer to the prayers of Fredonius, as some of our historians have supposed, or whether it happened just in the ordinary course of events. But in my humble opinion, in which I am confident of the support of all our great and popular men, to enter upon such inquiries, investigations, and metaphysical subtilities in a history of a civil empire, is "to mix, very improperly, civil and religious things together." I know it may be said, and has been said, "that much depended on the salvation of Fredonius and his ships; even the founding of the empire of Bawlfredonia—that heaven governs the tempests—that he sent **Fredonius** to discover this land—that he preserved him from the warring elements—that he answers the prayers of his children; and the answering of the prayer of the commodore, in this case, was preparing the way for founding a vast commonwealth."

But to all this I reply, that "we must not mingle civil and religious things together." A great king, or a great admiral ought not to be mentioned on the same page with religion, for two weighty reasons: First, It would be mixing civil and religious things on the plane of the same page, when they should be separated by huge mountains; and by such unnatural union, a notion might be encouraged, that kings and admirals should, as kings and admirals, be subject to the Almighty. What a preposterous idea for any *philosopher* to maintain! Second, Kings and admirals rarely have any religion; I acknowledge this a great evil; but I cannot admit what has been suggested by some illiberal folks, that the separation of religion and politicks by huge mountains and vast oceans, has been the cause of the impiety of our great men. Although it is true that heaven directs the concerns of empires, as well as individuals, we ought not to mention it, at least, in a grave historical work of the kind which I am now writing. I beg pardon of posterity for troubling them with so much on this subject. I say *posterity*, for I know my cotemporaries will pardon me, having witnessed lately, an attempt by almost the whole church of Bawlfredonia, to mingle church and state affairs. But more of this hereafter.

I might also inquire whether, as our great historians have asserted, and our philosophers affirmed, this storm was emblematical, typical, figurative, and ominous of the storms of faction which were to rage in Bawlfredonia, tearing the oars off the sides of the national ship, loosening its joints, tearing to pieces its cordage; the thunder and lightning—of war; the noise of windy political orators—of the separation of ****: a hiatus in the manuscript.

Although there may be some analogies traced here, I beg leave to offer one insurmountable objection to this theory. The great admiral who directs our national ship, cannot be suspected of praying to heaven to save the state in the storm. At least, I have never heard of his praying aloud, nor even in a whisper. I rather conclude he thinks it unnecessary, as he has said in one of his publick speeches, that, "our cause is so good a one, and we are such good people, heaven must save us."* Now if the

* Although, until the present day, I have not heard of our admiral praying, yet since closing this history, I have heard of his commanding others to pray. Being engaged in a most disastrous and ill conducted

E

analogy fails in this very important point, I say it must be thought a great straining of facts to extend their meaning so far as some writers have done.*

But leaving off these digressions, concerning curious metaphysical subtilities which have no relation to our affairs in a practical light, as beneath the dignity of history, I shall proceed to describe the appearances of the country, which lay in full view of the ships. I have said that to the north-east, a large bay opened.

The shores which enclosed this bay as far as the eye could reach, rose to a moderate height, by a gentle acclivity, except in a few places, where white

---

voyage, which he was resolved to prosecute, in opposition to the united opinions of his best seamen, to silence the murmurs on board, he ordered the chaplain to collect the crew, and join in publick prayers for a favourable wind to waft them back to their native shores. But, whilst the unsuspecting chaplain and crew were offering up their prayers for the favourable gale, our crafty admiral, aided by a Hindostan atheist, was engaged in altering and obliterating the figures upon an old chart, to aid him in deceiving the pilot, and conducting the ship in a different direction.—*Thwackius.*

* It may be thought that Thwackius here anticipates his facts, and breaks in upon the laws of historical writing. I affirm that this is one of his greatest beauties. His carrying the reader back to the ancient days of Fredonius, where he describes, in such glowing colours, the storm. To let the reader take a peep at futurity, is something like prediction. It charms him, and whets his appetite. I will further remark, that we may felicitate ourselves that the storm which assailed Columbus did not meet him until he was on his return to Europe; so no one can possibly imagine any thing portentous to us in the matter. Our remarkable exemption from the *storms of faction*, from *windy orators, &c.* puts the matter beyond all doubt.—*Am. Trans.*

cliffs ascended to the height of about three hundred feet, and extended, generally, about half a mile along the margin of the bay. The tops of these cliffs were crowned with lofty pines, waving in a gentle breeze, which still lingered in the rear of the tempest. The fronts of these rocky castles were variegated with larch, fir and pine shrubs, which were planted in the fissures of the rock. The intermediate grounds were covered with waving forests of the tallest trees. The esculus flava was clothed with its clusters of flowers, and spangled the grove. A thousand wild flowers imparted their hues to the surface of the ground, blooming around the margin of the forest. The border of shrubbery between this flowery carpet and the grove which it skirted, was adorned with leaves and flowers, which seemed to vie with each other, and the grove and flowery lawn, in beauty. It was in the month of Floreal,* when nature puts on her brightest robes. An innumerable variety of birds saluted with notes, soft, shrill, and loud, the returning morn, which disclosed the beauties of nature, freshened by the preceding rains. The rising mists were stealing away over the lovely landscape, or hovering around the brow of the cliff. Far distant, in majesty and beauty, rose a chain of moun-

* Answering to our November, which is the spring in the regions of Bawlfredonia and New Holland.—*Fr. Trans.*

tains, extending to the west further than the eye could reach. The rising sun gilded, just now, their summits. The deer bounded through the shrubbery, and the rabbit skipped on the flowery lawn. The wind is entirely lulled. Not a breath stirs the leaves. The waves break on the rocks, and there dying away in hollow murmurs far up the bay. The tattered sails hung motionless. The sailors in pensive, but luxuriant delight, stood with folded arms, gazing upon the enchanting scenery, and lifting up their souls in pious adoration to the great author of these beauties. Commodore Fredonius was in his cabin, making a record of the passing events, laying his plans for the day, and offering his morning devotions to the God who had preserved him; when suddenly, from behind a lofty white cliff, at no great distance, shot out a canoe, loaded with the native wild children of this Eden of the south.

Commodore Fredonius was immediately on deck, and ordered his people to treat the native inhabitants of this strange land, with every mark of kindness. This was his standing order on all such occasions. The canoe soon approached the ship, and was rowed round it, without any tokens of fear or distrust. The natives were of a copper colour, tall, straight, and of a serene countenance and noble aspect. Most of them wore no clothing, except the skins of strange animals about their loins. One of the persons who sat in the canoe had his head ornamented with a tuft of feathers of the most gaudy colours, and wore a loose robe of skin, covered with a great variety of figures, and ornamented with numerous appendages, tassels, tufts, and jingling trinkets. His mien, his dress and stature, indicated that he was a person of no mean rank.

He was brought on board, and several presents made him. In return, he invited Fredonius to land and visit him in his wigwam palace. The invitation was accepted. The common sailors could not be restrained. They hastened on shore, where the untaught children of the groves shewed them every mark of friendship and hospitality. Vegetables, viands, and preserved fruits, were presented to the commodore and his crew, with the most profuse liberality. The females were gay, cheerful, and though of a dark complexion, many of them were beautiful. Fredonius had no small difficulty to restrain his men within proper bounds, in their intercourse with the female part of the natives. Some symptoms of discontent soon began to manifest themselves amongst the males. It was plain that they disapproved of any familiarity with their wives or daughters, who were soon removed from the shore, and conducted to a place of greater security.

Fredonius looked upon the aborigines as the rightful possessors of the soil. He touched nothing without permission from the king, who was called Tecoghteranego.

Some of the crew were employed in refitting the shattered ships, others in keeping guard, and the whole committed to the care of the first captain; while, with permission from the Indian king, and accompanied by guides, Fredonius, and some of his people from each ship, set out on a tour of discovery. He found the country to correspond entirely with the indications presented at first view on the margin of the bay. Numerous savages of various tribes, and many towns were discovered. Every where the same hospitality and kindness was displayed by the natives. Wild fowls and animals in endless profusion and variety, sported around them in groves more lofty and luxuriant than any which they had before witnessed in Hindostan, or the intermediate islands. Brooks, or rivers, flowing from the distant mountains, or issuing from the surrounding hills, meandered through the forests. In these streams, as clear as chrystal, thousands of fishes, beautiful and of delicious flavour, desported. Fredonius was so respectful to the rights of the ancient but rude lords of the soil, that he did not even permit his men to angle for these fish without their permission.

Every thing gave the greatest pleasure to Fredonius, except that these hospitable people were utterly ignorant of the true God, and the manner of obtaining his favour. On his return to the wigwam of king Tecoghteranego, he found a fire kindled, and a female standing before it with her hands bound, and her head crowned with garlands, in the midst of a vast concourse of people. Upon inquiry, he was informed that during the late tempest, king Tecoghteranego had his castle laid in ruins. That a general alarm had prevailed, and that he had vowed to sacrifice one of his little daughters to the evil spirit, who he imagined had brought on the tempest, provided he would cause it to cease. The little girl, standing before the fire, was the child devoted.

Fredonius expostulated with the king against this sacrifice, but all in vain, until at length he gave him to understand, that unless he would relinquish his design, the sun should cease to shine upon the earth. It happened that on that day there was to be an eclipse of the sun, visible at that place. Fredonius made out to protract the negociation until the eclipse began to appear. Tecoghteranego and the assembled multitude, were filled with the deepest consternation. It was instantly spread abroad that the strange white people had caused the sun to go out, because the king was about to sacrifice his daughter.

The barbarous design was laid aside, and every mark of honour bestowed upon Fredonius, who, they began to think, was a god. As soon as the king declared that the sacrifice was given up, and the girl restored to her mother, Fredonius informed him that the sun should soon begin to shine again. At its appearance the most frantick joy was manifested. Since that time there has never been known an instance of human sacrifice being offered up by the natives of this country.

Having satisfactorily explored the country, repaired his ships, and laid in a plentiful supply of sea stores, he set sail for Hindostan, from the banks upon which he first landed, and which he named Asylum Harbour.

His return voyage was prosperous. I shall not trouble the reader with particulars.

Amongst other articles found in the neighbourhood of Asylum Harbour, was gold dust, of which as much was procured by the sailors, with the permission of Tecoghteranego, as was sufficient to enrich them. The knowledge of this circumstance soon excited numerous adventurers, to unite and fit out another expedition to Asylum Harbour. In one of the vessels of this second expedition, embarked a noisy young man, named Bawlfredonius. He possessed a little learning, but was poor and profligate.

By flattery and intrigue, and pretending to know a great deal of metals, especially gold, he prevailed upon the company of merchants, who had fitted out the squadron, to permit him to go on board as a mineralogist, and they even promised him high wages. I scorn to relate the particulars of the voyage:—I shall not pollute my page with the name of the commander. By the help of copies of the maps and journals of Fredonius, which had been purloined, they made out, after a long voyage, to reach Asylum Harbour, where they killed the deer, and other wild game, without asking permission of king Tecoghteranego—took by force all the trinkets they found upon the natives, debauched the women, and when the men offered to make resistance, destroyed their corn fields and fruit trees, and burnt down towns and villages, to the number of twelve, reducing a flourishing country to *"smoking ruins;"* declaring, at the same time, that they were heartily sorry to have been compelled to such measures. However, they comforted themselves, and appeased their consciences, (if they had any,) with a declaration, that the people, whose property they destroyed, were savages; and deserved to have their towns burnt, because they had been so untaught as to object to a free intercourse with their females. It was asserted that women ought to be held in common, and that for any

F

one man to appropriate to his sole use a woman, who was capable of making many happy, was an unpardonable sin, inasmuch as it tended to decrease *"the sum of human happiness."* Their colour was also pleaded as an excuse; "how could they expect better treatment, when they were so wicked as to be the colour of copper, which metal is known by alchymists to be poison." These were the arguments of Bawlfredonius, who, like one of his descendants, that I shall have occasion to mention hereafter, was a great pretender to the science, or the art, of alchymy. Taking a ground very different from that of his son of the twentieth generation, he affirmed that the *** of the males, made the females lawful spoil. How far these arguments were deemed conclusive by his countrymen is uncertain. At all events, nobody made much noise about the burning of savage towns, though, if in the wars of Hindostan, a town happened to be burnt, there was a prodigious uproar; which, as a historian and a man, I am very far from condemning. And I must express my abhorrence of burning the houses, and destroying the corn and fruit trees of poor savages; thus reducing to misery, thousands of innocent women and children.

Those who fitted out the expedition bestowed great applause upon the perpetrators of these abominable crimes, for their bravery, as they were pleased to term it, in reducing, to proper subjection, the women of Asylum Harbour, burning their houses, and other noble exploits. Upon the return of this expedition, Bawlfredonius published a book, (written, as he himself informs us, with a particular view to the edification of his children,) giving an account of his pretended discoveries, extolling the naked beauties, and fascinating charms of the *"unsophisticated children of nature;"* and what may be deemed surprising, even related his own burnings, and with much sang froid, philosophized upon the "smoking ruins," which marked his footsteps through this once happy land. I say *his own,* for he was foremost in the work of destruction.

He never mentioned the name of Fredonius, and as might be expected from his name, kept a most outrageous *bawling* about his adventures. If any one mentioned the name of Fredonius, in a company where this bawler was present, he did not fail to rave and storm about, what he audaciously called, his impositions. He would swear most horribly, for he was a very profane man, that Fredonius had never seen Asylum Harbour. He took great pains to circulate his book—he courted the great by fawning and flattery—the literary by pretending to letters and taste—the vulgar by swearing, gambling, and getting drunk with them, and the *** by debauchery. His

fame spread from the Ganges to the Indus, and to
the great mountains of Tibet. The great, mighty,
and potent emperor of the Moguls, sitting under a
canopy, and ruling over an hundred thousand provinces, (as he said,) sent for Mr. Bawlfredonius, and
heard him bawl about his discoveries. The great
and mighty continent of the south, was styled
BAWLFREDONIA. This was greatly to be deplored, but what followed was infinitely worse. He
fawned upon the courtiers about the palace of the
great Mogul, gained their favour, and employed his
whole influence to persuade them, and through them
the emperor, that Fredonius was a very dangerous
member of the state. That he had embraced the
Christian faith, had formed the most wicked plots
against the commonwealth, had laid a plan to seduce the subjects of the emperor to migrate to the
continent in the south, which himself, (Bawlfredonius,) had discovered.

He was seconded by the company of merchants,
who did not fail to give plenty of money to the courtiers, which carried all before it. In short, a decree
was issued to apprehend the good and great Fredonius, and carry him to Delhi, the capital of the empire. When the messenger, who was the bearer of
this decree, arrived at Seringapatam, Fredonius was
out upon a second voyage to Bawlfredonia; for alas!
I must call this land by that abominable name.

This voyage was a very fortunate one. For though the unhappy natives fled in every direction at the approach of the ship, yet no sooner did they discover that Fredonius was present, than king Tecoghteranego sent an embassy to him with an account of all that had been done by the banditti, who had visited the continent with desolation in his absence. "The woods," said they "withered at their approach. The deer hid in the brakes. The birds ceased to sing. Blood was in their hands and in their hearts. Didst thou send them?—or comest thou to condemn all the wickedness they did?—Wilt thou take us to thy bosom?"

To all this Fredonius gave such answers as was highly satisfactory. Though the common people were shy, and even the king had some fears and suspicions; the old friendship was revived. Fredonius kept his men in the strictest subordination. He had learned, on his first visit, the taste of the natives, and had supplied himself abundantly, with such articles as he knew would be highly gratifying to them and promotive of their comfort. These articles were distributed profusely by Fredonius, among Tecoghteranego and the princes and people who visited him. They were chiefly articles made of iron, such as hoes, hatchets, knives, nails, &c. The memory of the injuries sustained from Bawlfredonius and his lawless

crew, was in a great measure forgotten. Such articles as would be productive of profit by conveying
them to Hindostan, were procured by equitable ex-
changes, especially gold dust. The coast was explored to the south, several hundred miles, by captain Blackmoreland, who commanded one of the
ships belonging to Fredonius's squadron. By him
the great bay of Blackmoreland was discovered,
which, on his return, was called BLACKMORELAND
BAY, after his name. While at Asylum Harbour,
and during the absence of captain Blackmoreland,
Fredonius was employed in imparting instructions
relative to the culture of the ground, and some fruit
trees, of which he had brought with him the seed;
and in the manner of rearing some domestic animals
which he had brought with him to supply the natives, for whom he cherished a paternal affection.
He also imparted to them instructions on moral subjects, and a few plain precepts and doctrines of
Christianity. All things, when Fredonius left them,
seemed to be in a fair train for civilizing and evan-
gelizing this people. He returned to Seringapatam,
after a most prosperous voyage, in all of twenty
months. His vessels were laden with the richest
products of the southern climes, especially rare
plants and animals.

No sooner did he set his foot on shore, hoping to

meet the applause of all his compatriots, and repay the favours of his benefactors, than he was arrested, and dragged like a felon to Delhi; where, without a hearing, he was thrown into a loathsome dungeon, in which, in a short time, he breathed his last, under a load of irons, suffocated by the noxious air of the filthiest cell!! ***

Bawlfredonius was enjoying the tables and the favours of the great; having given his name to a vast continent. Good men, however, regarded him with abhorrence. No sooner was it known that Fredonius was dead, than he had many advocates who exerted themselves to do justice to his memory, to which a monument was erected in Delhi.*

Bawlfredonius soon found himself exposed to contempt; his conduct having been exhibited in its true colours by some of the friends of Fredonius. In order to escape from the publick indignation, he embarked in a vessel for Bawlfredonia. But no sooner had he made his appearance on shore, at Asylum Harbour, than Tecoghteranego placed an ambush for him. He was seized and hewed to pieces by one of the hatches which Fredonius had left there for other purposes. Thus ended this man his infa-

---

* This is a tribute of respect seldom paid in Hindostan, and which the rulers of this country have never paid to the memory of the GREATEST AND BEST of our heroes and statesmen, although it has long been demanded by the voice of every *patriot* in the nation.—*Thwackius.*

mous life, but to the disgrace of our country, his
name still lives.

I should not have spent so much time in deve-
loping the character of Bawlfredonius, but that there
is such a striking resemblance between some parts of
his character, and that of one of his descendants, who
was afterwards a king of this country. And some
have even supposed that the circumstance of his
name being impressed upon this southern world, has
had some effect in making us a noisy, vociferous,
talking, and *bawling* people. It has even been alledged that this circumstance has had an influence
upon our national character, in producing a similarity
to that of Bawlfredonius. But could any thing be
more fanciful, I may say more extravagant? It is
true we do bawl no little upon a variety of subjects,
especially respecting the superiority of our political
institutions over those of every other nation. But
then all other nations do precisely the same. Further, I do not question that some people, as will appear in this history, make use of means to prefer
themselves, pretty similar to that which Bawlfredonius used. But if they did not use such means, how
would they get into places of eminence? If they did
not, the principle of *"change and exchange of office"*
could not be supported. Bad men would not otherwise be brought to such condign disgrace. Had not

Bawlfredonius been exalted to that *"bad eminence,"* he could not have covered himself with *infamy so illustrious.* This will also appear in the most glowing colours, in the case of his renowned descendant, the *philosophical, alchymical* *** producing king.

G

FRAGMENT II.

When the Christian religion was introduced into Hindostan, which was not long before the time of
Fredonius, perhaps in the days of his father, it gave
great offence to the brahmins.   They stirred up the
emperor to inflict civil pains upon all who would embrace what they held to be worse than heresy.   The
emperor, by and with the advice of the grand lama,
considered himself entitled and capacitated to decide
on all matters of faith.   He was remarkably haughty,
opinionated, and cruel, as was his whole family.
Henry Mogul was on the throne when the Christian
religion was introduced. Christians were soon attacked with fire and faggot. Thousands were put to death
to gratify the brahmins.   There was no rest in the
kingdom.   Yet the true religion gained ground with
the greatest rapidity. Those who professed it had
their heads chopped off, were burnt at the stake, or
delivered over to wild beasts. Thus persecuted in
their native land, a few Christians, in order to free
themselves at once and for ever from their oppressors,
resolved to migrate to Bawlfredonia.

They provided a large ship, provisioned her, and
set sail. But not being the most expert seamen, it

was only, after encountering incredible hardships, they arrived at **Asylum Harbour.** They were kindly received by the natives, from whom they purchased a large tract of land, adjoining the harbour. They soon cleared fields, planted orchards, and reared flocks. They were a moral, industrious, and devout people. Others of the same character followed, and they prospered beyond all example. Their children tread in the footsteps of their fathers.

The emperor, who at first knew nothing of all these matters, was as length informed that his subjects had planted an extensive colony in Bawlfredonia. His counsellors were collected.—One spoke as follows:—

"These dogs of Christians ought not to be permitted in your majesty's dominions! Now Bawlfredonia is a part of your empire. Every place in which a subject of the great Mogul, immortal and sublime! ruling over thousands of provinces, and sitting under a canopy! sets his feet, is your property. You have a right to prescribe its modes of faith. I would even advise to have all the copper-coloured people to adopt our religion, or chop a few of their heads off, like cabbage heads; or I would burn them in faggots like sheaves of straw. I would cause the flame of their fires to blaze up to heaven. Send me and I shall destroy all the Christians, and either convert, at once, the natives to the Brahminical faith, or I will fatten the earth with their carcasses."

The emperor, who was rather fatigued with the work of murder, especially as he began to imagine that the ghosts of the dead visited him at night, and troubled his dreams—was observed to draw down his huge black eye-brows, while this bloody fellow was making his harangue. Another immediately arose and spoke to the following effect:—

"I do not presume to question the right of your most exalted majesty, the sun of the world! the emperor of thousands of provinces, and sitting under a canopy, to direct the faith of all nations! He is an enemy to all good government who would dare to doubt about this matter. But your most exalted majesty may, if you please, withhold your hand from the slaughter of those who are obstinate, when they are beyond many oceans, as the people of Asylum Harbour are. They may not have it in their power to do any great injury to the holy religion of your great empire. They will soon become rich, and if your most exalted majesty shall so determine, they can then be killed, and their wealth seized. But, in the meantime, they will gather gold dust, and we can either seize it by force, have it brought off in our vessels, or in some way make it travel into the sublime coffers of your very exalted majesty. I advise to be crafty with them. Pretend to favour them. Have a proclamation issued, forbidding any one to injure or disturb them, and giving them to understand, that they are considered, by your imperial majesty, as the lords of the soil. It will make them more industrious; we will thus make more out of them; and, in time, we can take away their privileges, with or without form."

The emperor being prodigiously avaricious, this speech pleased him mightily. As the speaker went on, a smile was sometimes seen to dart across his dark and surly visage. He arose from his throne, and strutting in awful royalty, like the royal tiger, about the hall, pronounced with emphasis:—"These unholy dogs, who have fled to Asylum Harbour, ought to die, every man of them; but I am resolved to be merciful, and so I order the last counsel given to be followed without delay."

Proclamation was accordingly made that the people of Bawlfredonia might stay where they were, and that as much land as they could get and cultivate, should, for the present, be considered as their own. ***

Under this proclamation all things went on in the new world, in the south, as it was sometimes called, with wonderful success. Hundreds went over every year, and the natural increase was almost miraculous.

The general opinion in Hindostan, especially amongst the nabobs, was, that all who emigrated to Bawlfredonia, became savages immediately after their arrival.

I have not here followed precisely the chronological order. If I had, the settlement of a colony at Blackmoreland Bay would have been mentioned before that at Asylum Harbour. However, I had important reasons for this apparent want of attention to the order of time. I leave my reader to conjecture what they were. Such exercise of the invention, when a historian can give it, becomes one of the most pleasing sources of enjoyment in historical reading. I know my business too well to explain every thing. I shall proceed to my narration.

The next year after captain Blackmoreland discovered Blackmoreland Bay, it was resolved to plant a colony at that place. This was carried into effect about thirteen years before the first emigrant settled in Asylum Harbour. It was planned by a very respectable nabob of Hindostan, to whom the emperor gave a charter.

The gentleman's design was to collect the profligate sons of those nabobs who were willing to part with them, and thus purify the country from its dregs. Large offers were made to such persons. Many of them assembled forthwith.—They had stars, garters, swords, &c.* such as their fathers wore. It would have made any one laugh heartily to see the way in which these gentry marched, with huge strides, along the beach, about the time of embarkation. They swore, tossed up their noses, and bade any one of their lower casts, who would accost them, to kiss ***: (a hiatus in the manuscript,) and proceed to cane him. They could be kept under no kind of government, during their voyage, nor after they arrived in Bawlfredonia.

The principal undertaker, the nabob of Patriagom, endeavoured, by reason, to reduce them to some kind of order. They would hear no reason. They said they were formed to rule, and they would rule. That the world was made for them only, they affirmed to be a truth. When the nabob was about buying the soil from the Pawtan Indians, they called him a fool to his teeth, and reasoned in the following manner, to prove that the natives had no right to the soil.

"They go naked, except the skin upon their loins; they are of an ugly colour; they are too straight and tall; they have no beards nor whiskers.—They do not live by agriculture, but by the chase; they do not worship Brahma; they have never obtained a

* These terms are not in the original exactly as I translate them. I use terms merely corresponding.—*Traducteur*.

right from either the grand lama, or the emperor
of Hindostan; their language is downright gibberage;
and finally, their faces are too flat."

All this was accompanied by a thousand oaths,
not important to be related in this place. However,
the nabob went on in his own way. Land for the
site of a town, some fields, &c. was purchased, and
paid for.—A town was laid out and called Nabobsburgh, and a system of laws was formed for the colony.

These and other matters adjusted, the nabob set
sail for Hindostan, leaving his colony to its destiny.
A few houses had been built in the town, and a few
acres of ground cleared previously to his departure.
To these no other improvements were afterwards added by his colonists; but on the contrary, the build-
ings were permitted to fall into ruins, and all things
were soon turned topsy turvy. The young nabobs
were both too proud and too lazy to work; and without labour there was no getting forward honestly
there, nor indeed any where else, when people were
poor.

What was to be done? The natives must be
plundered, which was done with the greatest heroism. Their grain was seized by violence, their venison was torn away by force from their wigwams,
and what was worse, the young nabobs seized their

wives and daughters and carried them away, as the Romans did the Sabines.* The savages were enraged beyond all endurance.—They resolved upon the most signal vengeance. As their manner is, they continued to wear the semblance of friendship, while they were hatching the deepest and direst plot that ever exploded. A general combination was formed of all the tribes as far to the north-west as the mountains. Arrow points were sharpened, knives were whetted, stone hatchets and iron hatchets were rectified, blood was drawn from their arms and drunk, in the midst of the most tremendous oaths and execrations that they would exterminate the whole of the white robbers, as they emphatically called our forefathers.

At mid-day, when all was silence, the few that would labour being in the fields, and the young nobility lolling upon their couches, and fanning themselves, for the day was hot, the savage war-scream burst from every hill and dale.—Had I a thousand tongues, and a pen of iron, I could neither tell nor write the number of the heroes of Bawlfredonia who, on that dreadful day, assembled their forces.—Historick muse recount the names of a few of the leaders;

* I do not know how Thwackius got this intelligence respecting the Romans. It is a deep and abstruse point, well worth inquiring into; only I suspect Traducteur slipped this comparison in without the authority of the original.—*Am. Trans.*

H

for thou alone canst tell. There were chieftains, Sastageretsy, Arrigh Kalihen, Alowateany, Towigh Towighraano, Gighdageghraano, Jerrenta Lynago, Tecumsehaganah—the old. Fierce and dreadful was their aspect.—Tell muse, who first, who last, was slain. *** Multa desunt. ****

Thus heaven destroys those who violate the rights of humanity. But some good men, honest, sober, and brave, fell defenceless, which we must record with compassion. As to the savages, their conduct was cruel; but, poor wretches, they were untaught.

Amongst those who survived the slaughter, were some who had made profession of religion, without having at any time known or felt the emotions of vital piety. They had been content to be called by the name of Christians, without practising any of the virtues of Christianity. Deeply humbled by the severe chastisement inflicted upon them, in mournful silence they proceeded to gather together the mutilated bodies of their slaughtered countrymen. A solemn fast was, for the first time, proclaimed in Nabobsburgh. The remains of the dead were deposited in a common tomb in the centre of the town, and a church erected upon the spot. For some time publick worship was regularly attended upon Sundays, and some of the young nabobs would occasionally talk of penitence for their past sins, and exhibit some symptoms of amendment. But the humility of a Christian life was too much opposed to their ideas of their own importance, and their sensual appetites soon became too strong for the restraints of virtue and religion. Some, however, became truly pious and devout, and many of their posterity have maintained the same character, down to the present day.

The Blackmoreland colony would now have been utterly ruined, and Bawlfredonia probably abandoned for ever, had not fresh supplies been at this moment received from Hindostan. The proprietor, indeed, who received the first charter, had been cheated by the emperor's ministers; but others had taken his place, who were active men, and resolved to prosecute their settlement.

The company now formed, bethought themselves of the propriety of sending out clergymen to civilize, and if possible, christianize the wild young men who had escaped the late carnage, and those who yearly flocked to the southern world, to mend their shattered health and fortunes. These clergymen were of great use;—though some of them, as they had their pay made sure by the company, soon became careless, and no better than they should be.

Perhaps I should have mentioned sooner, that a very remarkable weed was found in Bawlfredonia, which had never been heard of in Asia. STINKUM-

PUFF was the name given to it by the natives, and which it still retains. It was a kind of poison, of the most disagreeable taste and smell, and appearance, insomuch that no one, even of the Indians, ever presumed to cook or eat it in the way of sallad or greens. The young nabobs, who were remarkably fond of singularity, with many execrations upon all who would dare to think differently, pronounced its taste and smell most exquisite. To make good their words, as far as possible, they rolled up huge balls, larger than hen's eggs, and kept them in their cheeks. They also rolled together the leaves, clapped fire to one end, and stuck the other in the side of their mouths.

This apparatus gave their heads the appearance of burning mountains. Huge columns of smoke issued from their mouths, darkening the atmosphere all around them. The sulphurous steam which issues from other volcanoes, does not smell half so offensively. Streams of fiery coloured lava flowed in vast and impetuous torrents down their chins, blasting, in its course, the downy beards of the petit maitres, and deluging fire-hearths, carpets and floors, to the great discomfiture of the whole housewife tribe.

The leaves and stems were also ground to powder, producing a reddish dust, which the nabobs rammed into their noses, thereby throwing the whole body into an agitation, as great as that produced when the fabled giant turns himself under the volca-nick mountain.

One would have supposed that such a filthy and barbarous custom, of metamorphosing the head and the human body into such forms and *chamœras dire*, would have found votaries no where but in the wild woods of some savage country.—But no, it soon found its way to Hindostan. Let a few nabobs adopt a practice, no matter how absurd, and the whole country soon follows. The rage, in short, for this noxious weed, as far as I can learn, became uni-versal. This desire for novelty, and this fondness for following the fashions of the nabobs, has not de-creased in Bawlfredonia.

Not many years ago a saltatorean swindler and gambler, of great celebrity, named Apollyon, stood in the pillory, and was banished from his native country for some dashing feats in his way of trade. He made out to bear off with him a considerable pro-perty, a splendid equipage, and a beautiful courte-zan, and fixed his residence in the capital of Bawl-fredonia.—His neck and ancles having been much injured by the shackles of the pillory, which had occasioned large protuberances upon those parts, he made out to cover these deformities, by sticking his shanks into a huge pair of wide boots, much resembling a pair of fire buckets; and by folding round his neck a pad of cotton, rolled up in three and a half yards of white cambrick, which projected four inches beyond the point of his chin. His companion, of the frail sisterhood, who now passed for the countess Apollyon, having nothing which she desired to hide, and resolving to *astonish the natives*, by a full view of her charms, appeared in publick, dressed, or rather undressed, in a single thin robe of saltatorean gauze, which encircled without hiding her body, leaving her arms and shoulders entirely bare.

As the Bawlfredonians have a great partiality for foreigners, especially such as have fled from the gallows or pillory in their native country, and in re-venge, abuse it heartily, the count and countess did not fail to meet with much attention in the capital of Bawlfredonia. The queen, who in the early part of her life had moved in an humble, though respectable sphere, and had been, by her worthy mother, confined to a plain drab coloured dress, without gauze or trim-mings, having, by a lucky hit, ascended the throne, was resolved to indemnify herself for the privations suffered in her youth. Although she was past the me-ridian of life, and rather corpulent, yet she was resolv-ed, in every point, to be up to the tip of the fashions.

Upon the first appearance of the count and coun-tess Apollyon, in the levee of her majesty, many of the most respectable maids and matrons left the room, shocked at their indecent and disgusting appearance. But the queen was highly pleased with the rude beauty of the countess; and every petit maitre coxcomb and puppy, who danced attendance at her drawing room, was loud in the praise of thin robes, wide boots, and jutting pads.

At the next levee her majesty appeared in a thin robe, with naked arms and shoulders, surrounded by a numerous collection of animals in wide boots and huge neck-pads, bearing a striking resemblance to newly caught monkies and baboons. A few females were to be seen clad in thin apparel, with the points of their elbows exposed. It rather appeared that the mass of the female part of society felt some repugnance to the fashion; but the example of her majesty and her maids of honour, soon overcame all their delicate scruples. In less than a year, bare arms, bare shoulders, and thin transparent robes were all the ton amongst the ladies of high life, and low life too.

This lewd and indecent fashion was opposed by the virtuous and sober part of the community with great zeal. But the example of the court was too powerful for the voice of chastity and reason. The fashion daily gained ground, and many chaste and modest women, both young and old, rather than be pointed at for singularity, threw aside their petticoats, and exposed their delicate limbs to the chilling frosts and scorching sun. In consequence of such exposure, many thousands of the fairest daughters of Bawlfredonia, annually fell sacrifices to pulmonary complaints, rheumatisms, and other disorders, brought on by the want of clothing. Still, however, the fashion was persevered in, in spite of every expostulation, warning and suffering. It is probable the whole country would have been depopulated by this detestable fashion, had not a grave legislator proposed and carried a law, prohibiting, under severe penalty, all women, kept mistresses and common prostitutes only excepted, from appearing in publick, either in summer or winter, without a sufficient stock of clothing to cover their nakedness.

I shall now proceed to give the traditional account of the native Bawlfredonians, respecting the origin of stinkum-puff.

They say that, soon after the beginning of the world, a woman of benign aspect, came from the north-west, riding upon a cloud, and alighted upon the top of one of those high mountains which runs through the country. Having seated herself upon her base, she placed her right hand upon the ground towards the north-east, and her left to the south-west. In a voice like thunder, she called to the natives to "*come, and they should* FIND," and then fled away on the cloud. They hastened to the spot; and, where her right hand rested, they found corn; where her left rested, pulse; and, precisely under her posteriors, they found STINKUM-PUFF.

No matter how it originated; it was soon in universal demand as an article of commerce. The sails which wafted it to every land whitened every sea; and thousands every year fell sacrifices to its baneful effects.

The soil of Blackmoreland was found admirably adapted to its culture. The Blackmorelanders made their living by "*growing*" it.

So much have I thought necessary to premise relative to this wonderful plant, merely as a preface to the introduction of a stock of women, or ladies, into the Blackmoreland colony. It was found extremely difficult to sustain and increase the population without females. Some advised to take into partnership the aboriginal females. One, a princess, of uncommon virtue, was tried in that line, and found to succeed remarkably well, and to be useful in various ways, by securing the friendship of the natives, &c.*

* Her descendants have been eminent for their patriotism, their hatred of tyranny, and their keen and sarcastick wit. One of them has, of late years, filled some of the most dignified stations in our councils, and has often charmed our ears with his cutting and satirical oratory, at the

I

But this project was over-ruled, and *"after mature deliberation,"* it was resolved to import a ship-load for sale, which was done accordingly. As all trade was carried on in stinkum-puff, the females were sold for twice their weight of that plant, putting the lady twice in the scale, and weighing her against the stinkum-puff.

There was no disparagement intended by all this, and so there was no offence taken.

I forgot to mention, in the proper place, that an attempt was made, by some immoral people, to introduce the use of stinkum-puff into Asylum Harbour colony. But the Asylumonean council soon checked it, by decreeing—

"That whosoever should be legally convicted of wearing stinkum-puff between his teeth and cheek, or any where in his mouth, or burning rolls of it under his nose, or of ramming the powder into his nostrils, within ten miles of any dwelling house, should, for the first offence, pay a fine of ten pieces of silver; for the second, be imprisoned for one year; and, for a third, banished and his goods confiscated."

It will be perceived at once, that this amounted to a total interdiction, as it was probably intended.

The cultivation and the trade in this article,

---

expense of our late renowned and valiant king, Pigman Puff, and his sapient ministers.—*Thwackius.*

was not in the least affected by this "unkind and ungenerous decree" of the sister colony. No: Blackmoreland flourished, and carried on a very extensive trade for her age. Among articles of trade, some human beings were offered for sale in Nabobsburgh. But as this was an affair of some importance, and as we are interested in it to this very moment, I shall trace it back to its origin.

A people lived about the mouth of the great Mayhong, on very low grounds, where there were marshes of great extent, and a vast number of frogs. From their marshes, they were called Mudlanders. A certain great writer personified the whole nation very beautifully, by calling it Nicholas Frog. However, this is perhaps below the dignity of my history. I go on to state that the Mudlanders, who once possessed great virtues, and do still possess many, were prodigiously avaricious. They made their living chiefly by naval commerce. Their ships visited the southern seas in search of spices, and other articles of trade. They, at length, found a vast island, or rather peninsula, inhabited by a nation of people perfectly black. They either thought, or pretended to think, that the devil must have the sole government of those people who were of his own colour. It was said, that to make war upon the subjects of a king, was to make war upon himself.

As the devil, (Ahraman in the original,) ruled here,
they would make war upon him through his subjects; and at best, these people were savages; and as
great heroes had, in more instances than one, burnt
down savage towns, and slaughtered their inhabitants
en masse, there could be no harm in capturing a few
of those black animals, and exposing them to sale in
the common course of trade. Some scruples were
started, but war measures prevailed. A few har-
dened fellows, with axes and spears, and swords,
and long pikes, and huge knives, landed under cover
of some high bushes, and rushed upon a village, in
which there were a few old men, and a great number
of women and children, with about half a dozen stout
and resolute young men. The surprise of the towns-
people was infinite, at seeing, for the first time, white
faces, and all the war passions depicted upon them;
their hands also armed with instruments of death
the most frightful. The Mudlanders rushed into
the village, and seized the handsomest and strongest
of the females, and began to bind them. The young
men were roused; and, though altogether unprepared
for battle, resisted most manfully. The armed Mudlanders began to hew them down; their brains were
knocked out with the axes, their arms cleft off by the
swords, and their hearts pierced by the spears. A
dreadful cry was raised, and multitudes flocked in
from every part of the surrounding country.

In this attack, fifty women were murdered, twenty men were hewn to pieces, and forty children had their brains dashed out. One hundred were wounded, and twenty taken prisoners; twelve men and eight women. The prisoners were hurried on board the ship, loaded with irons, and stowed away like other articles of traffick.

The great object was to find the best market for the black captives. As it was well known that the colony of Blackmoreland Bay was, in a great measure, made up of young Hindostanese nabobs, who were not willing to labour, and had a great rage for stinkum-puff, it was resolved to try that as the market best adapted to the views of the Mudlanders. The vessel was despatched forthwith for Nabobsburgh, where they soon arrived, and offered their black prisoners of war for sale, to be kept as slaves to the end of the world.

On this important occasion a council was called of the principal citizens of Nabobsburgh, by the chief magistrate of the colony, in order to deliberate on the measures to be taken. Many were the wise speeches made that day. The principal speaker, in favour of legalizing this species of commerce, was Andrew Anthropophagus, esq. the tyger-hearted, who arose and addressed the assembly in *"winged words,"* to the following effect:—

"With permission of your excellency, and you my townsmen, I have been at the ship, and examined the animals which are there exposed to sale, by our good friends, the brave and benevolent Mudlanders. I am happy to inform you all, that those animals will serve a most valuable purpose, in raising our dearly beloved stinkum·puff. They have claws very much resembling human hands, and so constructed that I perceive it will be possible for them to handle a hoe. They also walk erect, upon what may be termed their hind feet; by which circumstance there will be less danger of their tramping down the stinkum-puff, when the plants are young and tender.

"They appear to be animals of a sagacious species, for they use, among themselves, something like articulate sounds; and they have, I am told, while on ship-board, learned to understand a few words of the Mudland language. Hence I conclude, we can so far teach them to manage our business, as that we may loiter in the shade and spend our whole time in the delectable business of eating, drinking, and ***

"Whereas, I fear that doubts have arisen, that perchance these animals may be human beings, of our brethren, whose complexions may have been changed from some unknown cause; and that, therefore, there may be some sin against heaven, and the rights of human nature in trafficking in human flesh and spirit; I do, with the leave of your excellency, consider these remarks as wholly irrelevant, and pro- ceeding from a narrow minded people, who have not been stained," (tinctured, probably he meant,) "with the *new philosophy,* which begins to be in vogue. Such scruples, though this remark may be rather new, started in an assembly strictly civil, sa- vours too much of a wish 'to jumble church and state affairs together:' [the governor frowns.] Even if they are men, our business is not to consider the sin, or the duty of the matter, but the policy. If that can be settled, we have no more to do. The church may think of the rest. But I say they are not men; they have no souls, or they would be white—for the soul is white, and of course makes the body white too.* Besides, will your excellency, and you my fellow-citizens, only consider that their hair is fright- fully frizled, and their noses not the shape of a man's nose. Their lips are too large, their legs of a strange shape, and—and—and—and why, I tell you again, they are black."

* A new sect of philosophers have contended, that the human soul, be- ing "*a species of fine spun matter,*" when first spoken into existence by the fiat of the Deity, has all the forms and organs of the human body, though of a most diminutive size. This soul, being thus formed and organized, afterwards, by its own exertion, expands into the upright and athletick figures, which walk abroad upon this mundane sphere under the name of man. How far this profound theory of procreation supports the reasoning of Anthropophagus, I leave to the decision of my philosophical readers.— *Thwackius.*

Being out of ideas, and out of breath too, he was obliged to sit down. There were bursts of applause from almost every part of the assembly. There were, however, two clergymen present, who both rose to speak against what they considered a most wanton and cruel outrage upon the rights of humanity. But they were hissed, and compelled to give over. The decree was passed to legalize the trade in human beings. The two clergymen were together when they went out of the hall of judgment.—One says to the other:—

"Brother, I see these poor people will be bought, had we not better purchase two or three a-piece; we can make their situation more comfortable; we can teach them religion; then they will be of some use to us." The other replied indignantly:—

"You see a man about to be murdered and robbed, and in order to prevent him from being tortured to death by beating, you determine to despatch him at once, by cutting off his head, to give him an easy death. Then *his money will be of some use to you,* so you will e'en take it." This reply produced no effect.

Parson Wordly, the other reverend gentleman in question, went forthwith, and was the highest bidder for a man and a woman. The other, parson Faithful, stood on the deck of the ship, and with a loud

voice related the manner of taking these poor crea-
tures captive, and denounced the vengeance of heaven against all who would dare to bid at the auction.
However, he was threatened with a mob, and compelled to desist. Anthropophagus purchased two
black women, whom he made both his slaves and
his concubines. His own children he sold from the
bosoms of these women, one every two years, as
soon as they were able to walk.

After this introduction of historical facts, I am
also tempted to believe that there was something
ominous in this country's having been called Blackmoreland. The Mudlanders soon employed a great
number of ships solely in this trade. The Hindostanese also embarked in it; and, in process of time,
the Blackmorelanders themselves, and even some of
the Asylumonians. The country was overrun with
the black people.

You might, in a few years after this trade was
introduced, have seen in Blackmoreland, people of
all colours, white, black, yellow, red, brown, gray,
and in short, every hue between perfect black and
white, which some philosophers say, embraces all
possible colours. In some districts, to be the father
of half a dozen of these party-coloured people, was
considered as the most valuable testimony of the
"perfectability" of a young nabob.

K

In a territory on the southern borders of Bawlfredonia, settled chiefly by emigrants from Saltatoria and Blackmoreland, the female posterity of this mungrel brood, called "QUARTER BLOODS," are, by their mothers, openly and publickly hired out to the young nabobs by the week, month, or year, for the purposes of prostitution.

Dancing associations have also been formed, in which all the males are white nabobs, and the females, all of the party-coloured tribe. These associations meet in the most publick parts of the chief city, and their meetings are at all times, and especially upon Sundays, most numerously attended.* Upon that day it is also usual to encourage the full blooded black slaves to collect together upon the commons, and there to exhibit the musick and dances of their native country, for the amusement and edification of the sons and daughters of their chaste and pious masters.

* These quarter blood balls are said to be held in high estimation, not only by the nabobs of the south, but by some of the dealers in notions, who have of late adopted the principles of the new philosophy. Their favourite dance, as described to me by a late traveller, resembles one which began to be in fashion about the time of my sailing from France, called "The Waltz."—*French Trans.*

FRAGMENT III.

*** Multa desunt: ***—not so. The two co-
lonies flourished beyond all former example. They
had spread themselves to the north, south, east and
west, over a vast extent of territory. The two colonies of Asylum Harbour and Blackmoreland, had
come together; and, indeed, had some disputes in relation to their respective boundaries. These, however, were amicably settled.

The character of the people was somewhat peculiar. The peasants were spread over the hills and
dales. They usually cleared a small spot of ground,
and this was cultivated in rather a careless manner;
but the fertility of the soil made up for deficiencies in
their mode of cultivation. A great portion of their
time was devoted to the chase. The great variety of
wild game produced in the woods of Bawlfredonia,
rendered this country, in a peculiar manner, the do-
main of Diana. The huntsmen would spend whole
months far from the abodes of men. By night they
slept in the open air. They traversed the woods the
distance of forty or fifty miles in a day, without any
other refreshment than the waters of the chrystal
brook. This rendered them as hardy as the ancient

Persians. Great bodily vigour was their peculiar attribute. They presented a broad back between the shoulders, and their lower limbs were inserted into a huge frame of bones, covered with brawny muscles. Withal, they were remarkable for agility and swiftness in all gymnastick sports. Every man thought himself equal to a king. They were, besides, a little rude. To take off their hat, even to a king, would have been esteemed a great courtesy, or rather condescension. If demanded, it would not have been done. Some even held it sinful to shew such a mark of respect *"to a fellow creature."* There were few poor amongst these our ancestors, and not many rich. A golden mediocrity was the common condition, particularly in Asylum Harbour. They were remarkable for truth and integrity. A man or woman, who would have forfeited his or her word, would have been disgraced for ever.

There was, however, a considerable dissimilarity between the people of the northern and those of the southern colony. In Blackmoreland, the slaves which were introduced, spoiled, in many instances, the morals of the youth; of course the men made out of these youths, were spoiled too.

There you might see *"young master"* raging and storming at the little Blackamore before either of them was four years old. The white child holding a whip over the black one, would curse and storm just as it had seen its father do when chastising the older slaves. Thus the child assumed the air of an emperor, and was a tyrant in reality. The habit of idleness also, in which the young men had time to indulge, and indeed, the old too, while the slaves wrought for them, produced the most noxious effects.

They were much addicted to gambling. People of the first fashion would spend whole days and nights in tossing about small ivory balls, with little pictures upon them, resembling toads, snakes, devils and Venuses, crying out "Toads for a shiner! snakes for a hundred! devils for a thousand! and beauties for a brace of curley heads."* Sometimes when a toad or a devil would turn up instead of a Venus, the losing party would storm, and rage, and swear, and damn Fortune for a fickle whore, whilst the winners would bless the pretty face of their toad or devil.

It was not uncommon to see the value of a whole year's labour of a slave risked upon a single turn of these balls. At other times, the slaves themselves would be betted; and it frequently happened that whole farms would be stripped of their labourers, and whole families reduced to beggary in the course of one night.

* A name by which they called their black slaves.—*French Trans.*

When gambling was first introduced, it was confined to a few nabobs of the higher orders; and, for a time, they plundered each other, according to what was termed, "the laws of honour;" but, in process of time, the members of the fraternity of "GREENSHANKS"* contrived to mix with the nabobs at the gaming table, and the race ground.

This fraternity was made up of the most dexterous sharpers, and the most audacious swindlers in the land. They practised all manner of juggling, and had invented certain signs, and a kind of gibberish by which they were known to each other at first sight, and enabled to unite their skill and dexterity in plundering the nabobs and gentlemen gamblers.

When a young nabob was fairly stripped of all his coin, and all his "curley heads," and reduced to a state of desperation, it was not uncommon for the Greenshanks to offer him admission into their society, and a participation in the secrets and plunder of the fraternity.

Some of the most thoughtless and extravagant of these young men, notwithstanding the evil courses in which they had indulged, still retained a sufficient

* From what I have heard of this society, they bear a striking resemblance to our Knights of Industry, and to the English tribe of Blacklegs. But the Greenshanks, in addition to their other villanous tricks, were great adepts in the art of counterfeiting coin, picking locks, and thieving.—*French Trans.*

sense of honour to reject such offers with horror and disdain. But too many were found ready to accept them, and to act as decoys in leading their unsuspecting associates to destruction. Many worthy and respectable parents were brought, in sorrow, to their graves by the infamy of their sons, who had learned their first lessons of vice at the gaming table.

For a time this vice seemed to infest all ranks in society, from the proud nabob to the shoe-black. Frequently you might find nabobs and chimney-sweepers, counsellors of state and negro-drivers, lawyers and hangmen, physicians and grave-diggers, horse-jockies and horse-thieves, all jumbled together upon the race course, or elbowing each other at the cock-pit, or gaming table.

Indulgence of the several appetites became too common. Eating, drinking, and wenching, were practised to a most ruinous extent. In the natural course of things, they adopted the most dangerous notions relative to morals. There were always some of the emigrants who held the pagan tenets which prevailed at Hindostan; but the greater body of those who emigrated were, or at least professed to be, proselytes to the Christian religion. However, the vicious indulgencies produced from slavery, required some palliative. As they were forbidden, in the holy scriptures, from having any carnal dealings with the black women, unless they would make them their wives, they took it into their heads to deny the divine authority of the Bible. Among those, however, who had embraced these scriptures, there was no little struggle e'er this was effected, or before they dared to go such lengths. For a long time the debauchees took every one his own course without any union or harmony. At length it was resolved to form their plans into a system. For this purpose, measures were taken to arrange themselves into a society, embracing all those *mettlesome* young men, who were desirous of setting the common opinions and feelings of society at complete defiance. Some dashing old men were also taken in. A night was appointed—the hour midnight. Peter Paunch was appointed president, and Lodowick Slanderburgh, secretary. The meeting being called to order, Oliver Ophicus, senior, rose to explain the objects of association, and spoke as follows:—

"Mr. President, I beg your indulgence, while I attempt to develope the designs of our collecting at this dark and silent hour. I need not state to this society that our rights have not only been invaded, but wrested from us. Our dearest enjoyments are abridged. If we drink to drunkenness, the most refined pleasure—if we embrace a ****, a most rational and dignified amusement—if we pass our time at the gaming table, the race course, or cock-pit, by which alone many of us can make our living—if we damn and swear, which renders us more consequential—if we break a promise to shew our independence—if we despatch only a turkey, two or three ducks, and a saddle of venison each, at a meal—if we shoot, in a duel, any impudent fellow who curls up his nose at our nabobship—if we kick, or turn out of doors, an old doating or peevish father or mother—if we seduce the wife or daughter of our patron, and thus gratify those passions which we feel to be most deeply implanted in our hearts by nature—we are stigmatized by the priests, fanaticks, and rabble of the colony as wine bibbers, whore-masters, gluttons, blasphemers, cheats, parricides, cut-throats, and a whole army of hard names, slanderous, in a high degree, to our fair characters.

"Now I make bold to affirm that this evil which has grown old amongst all, proceeds from the respect shewn to the book, called the Holy Bible. The grand object of our association will be, I presume, to diminish that respect for this book which has hitherto prevailed in society. But it requires the *"most mature deliberation"* to fix upon the measures which should be adopted. I would advise that the appearances of respect for the Christian religion should, for some time, be kept up; that is to say, in mixed com-

L

panies, amongst strangers and religionists. Let us
move with extreme caution, otherwise all our prospects are blasted for ever. Let all the blemishes in
the character of the clergy, be marked and magnified
upon every occasion. Let us court their society, and
present them all possible temptations, and never fail
to cite their vices as evidences against Christianity.
Ridicule every layman who presumes to pray, and
call rigid morality, bigotry and narrowness of soul.
Offer sly insinuations against particular portions of
the Bible; suggest doubts which may perplex and
stagger the faith of the illiterate, but avoid an open
avowal of hostility to the scriptures or religion. Let
us court young men, and infuse our liberal views into
their minds through the medium of the bottle, and
the raptures of unrestrained devotion to Venus. In
her temples we shall not fail to make proselytes.
Finally, let us, by secret measures, procure copies of
the works of those, who, in Hindostan, have written
against the Christian religion, to be circulated
amongst the people. They are fond of novelty, and
prone to adopt new systems, and we shall soon make
many converts. My brethren, this is my plan; I have
divulged it with freedom, as I am happy to find the
company is remarkably select."

Whilst Ophicus was thus speaking, Tom Anguish, a stay-maker and pamphleteer, who had late-

ly emigrated from Hindostan,* eyed him with indignation. On the brandy nose and ghastly bloated
face of the stay-maker were depicted the features of
a thousand fiends. He instantly rose, and proceeded
as follows:—

"Friends! countrymen! freemen! and fellow-citizens! I despise the meanness which could dictate
the measures recommended by brother Ophicus; it is
even with some reluctance I call him brother. No.
let us wage open war against these execrable, infernal principles; which, like so many chains, bind our
hands and feet!—these forgeries of the priests! I
swear by the shrines of Venus and Bacchus to pursue them, even with fire and sword, if possible, to
their extermination, and that of all their bigoted, hypocritical votaries.—I have done."

After much reasoning and expostulation on the
part of Ophicus, and the more artful members, Anguish was a little calmed.

---

* As the stay-maker will cut no inconsiderable figure in this history, it
may not be improper to inform the reader of the circumstance to which
our country was, in the first instance, indebted for his presence. Tom had
a wife in Hindostan; her friends alledged that he *laced* her too *tight*,
and laid on the whale-bone rather *heavy*. He spent at the grog-shop and
the club-room, more than he earned. To free her from his barbarity, and
the expense of maintaining a drunken husband, they purchased her freedom by paying him ten pieces of silver, providing him with a keg of rum,
and defraying the expense of his passage to Bawlfredonia. Upon a subsequent occasion, Tom was imported from Saltatoria in a national ship, by
order of king Tammany, "to prosecute his useful labours in this land of
liberty."—*Thwackius.*

As he was a good writer *adcaptandum vulgus*, it was resolved that he should seize some favourable occasion, and write two or three pamphlets upon the most popular themes, agreeably to the general principles of morality. And as soon as he should, by such publications, and the puffing of the society, acquire a sufficient stock of popularity, he should indulge his disposition for war, by some open and daring attack on the Bible and religion generally. To this he assented.

After closing *"their useful labours,"* they adjourned to a neighbouring tavern, where they indulged in eating and drinking, until most of the members were laid under the table. Such as were able to walk, after exulting over their vanquished companions, issued forth in search of other sport. A full score of slaves, of half blood, was added to the colony by the philo. sophical experiments of the members of the society, in the latter end of that night.

However, we are not to suppose that all the Blackmorelanders were of this depraved character. There were great numbers of excellent people in the colony, who deplored these evils, and did every thing in their power to check their progress. The very fury of the Bacchesian society, (for that was the name it assumed,) described above, affords evidence that there was much opposition to them.

The people of Blackmoreland were also generally hospitable in a very high degree. Even the
most profligate members of society seemed to pride
themselves in this virtue; and, no doubt, hoped it
would atone for all their vices. For however they
might pretend, their consciences informed them that
what they called free living was, in fact, vicious living. Even Tom Anguish, it is said, had at times
some sore twitches of conscience. But I do not
vouch for the truth of this assertion. The Blackmorelanders were also brave as a people. No
enemy might dare to attack them with impunity.

The Asylumonians were a sober, ploding, industrious, saving, and economical race. They would
rarely open their mind fully and plainly to any one;
yet they were extremely inquisitive. If a stranger
appeared amongst them, he was sure, if he would be
patient, to be asked ten thousand questions respecting his name, residence, business, &c. They had
churches in every little village; so devout were they
esteemed, that their chief town was called, by strangers, Puritanville, and it bears that name until
this day, as all my Bawlfredonian readers know.

Religion and religious topicks were discussed
among them with as much interest as political questions in Blackmoreland. Swearing, drunkenness,
gaming and debauchery, was scarcely known in that

colony; cheating was not so rare, especially amongst the dealers in notions.

When a bargain was made, it was esteemed most sacred. An Asylumonian, after having entered into a contract, would drive a cart laded with wooden bowls of his own fabrication from Puritanville to the most southern extremity of Bawlfredonia, scarcely halting day or night, rather than fail in performing a single article of agreement.

Indeed to row a boat, laded with *notions*, even to Hindostan; or drive a cart, with wooden ware, through every region of Bawlfredonia, was no uncommon achievement for the common people of Asylumonia.

Their carts multiplied to such extent, that there was usually two on every farm; one for plantation business, the other for foreign commerce; I mean Blackmorelandian commerce. Almost every creek and bay was crowded with boats, of various sizes, from Asylumonia; by means of which, every country on the south of Asia, and all the neighbouring islands, were laid under contribution. Though, at an early period, they would not suffer the use of stinkum-puff to be introduced into their settlements, nor the black people to be kept as slaves, yet, rather than their vessels should want employment, they would, sometimes, freight them with stinkum-puff

from Nabobsburgh to any port where it would sell.
On their return voyage they would not hesitate to
bring large cargoes of slaves, which they sold for as
high a price as possible, to the tyrants of Blackmoreland. Thence, though they made such unva-
ried opposition to the introduction of black slave
labourers, and black slave breeders, into their pro-
vince, yet stinkum-puff, in all its abhorrent forms,
was at length very generally used. The sailors became fond of it, and soon found means, while in port,
to evade the law. The captains of vessels were in-
fested by the contagion, and the evil spread over the
whole country with incredible rapidity. The law
against it was not formally repealed, but it soon became a dead letter. Even legislators and governors,
to the great scandal of the more sober part of the
community, indulged themselves in violating this
law. Notwithstanding these vices, which were productive of much evil, the people of the Bawlfredonian settlements were, upon the whole, in a highly
flourishing condition. Agriculture produced abundance of the fruits of the earth. The forest yielded
wood, in profusion, for all purposes. Manufactories were beginning to take root. Taxes were light,
and *demagogues* and *office-hunters* were unknown.
And, although the emperor of Hindostan had very
meanly and tyrannically laid their commerce under

great restrictions, yet it flourished to a most incredible extent, and its fame spread over the whole earth.

The emperor began to regard it with an eye of jealousy and avarice, and was resolved to humble its growing pride. He determined to place a king over the whole country, who should be tributary to him; also, to send over a whole herd of brahmins, who should have the tenth of all the produce of the soil, as they had in Hindostan, and to establish casts upon the model of those of his Asian empire; for these odious destructions had utterly disappeared in the new world of the South Sea. Every man was noble or ignoble there, in proportion to his own real or supposed value. However, as the Bawlfredonians had been found, on some former occasions, to be rather a mettlesome and intractable race; and as their known prowess made them not a little formidable, it was resolved to proceed with caution, and subdue them by piece-meal, as they did the lions of the south of Asia. The emperor, therefore, determined to abridge their enjoyments, at first in a few articles only, and as far as possible to prevent them from procuring the means of self-defence.

For this purpose the emperor passed an edict, prohibiting, under the severest penalties, all his subjects from exporting to Bawlfredonia, any great guns, swords, hatchets, gun-powder, flints, tents, blankets, or any other matter which might be useful in war.

Upon hearing of this edict the Bawlfredonians painted, and dressed up in the garb of the natives, some three or four hundred of their most active and daring young men, and despatched them in bark canoes and boats to one of the emperor's garrisons, on an island to the eastward of Puritanville.

Some of the young men, having gained admission, under pretence of bartering venison for glass beads, immediately knocked down the sentinels with their hatchets, and threw open the gates to their companions. These, *"by a sudden movement,"* rushing in, raised the war-whoop, seized the emperor's soldiers, and, binding them hand and foot, stowed them away in a corner of the fort.

In this *"durance vile,"* his majesty's troops were detained until all the great guns upon the battery, amounting to upwards of forty in number, together with a large store of gun-powder, shot, tents, blankets, &c. were conveyed to a place of safe keeping in Asylum Harbour. When the removal of the guns and stores was completed, some fishermen were sent to release the soldiers, who did not fail to represent to the emperor the great sufferings which had been inflicted upon them by "an overwhelming multitude of savages of the wilderness."

M

The Bawlfredonians, elated with their success, and forewarned of the mischief that was coming against them, spared no pains to prepare for resistance. Their flocks of sheep were increased to provide them with clothing and blankets. Their flax and hemp-fields were enlarged to furnish them with sail-cloth, field-frocks and tents. The caves of their mountains were explored for salt-petre; powder manufactories sprang up in every corner of their country, and their dealers in "notions" were despatched to the adjacent coasts and islands, to barter onions and stinkum-puff, for firelocks and cutlasses.

At this period it might be said of those people as of the Israelites of old, "In those days there was no king in Bawlfredonia, and every man did that which was right in his own eyes." Fortunately for the liberties of our country, every man did that which was right in the eyes of all prudent statesmen. And here I cannot but remark the great contrast between the conduct of these republican sages, and that of the late king Pigman Puff, who, whilst contemplating war, adopted every measure which could tend to deprive his subjects of the means of carrying it on to advantage.

Shortly before these occurrences, a numerous emigration had arrived in Bawlfredonia, from a beautiful little island on the north-east of Hindostan, called Bogland. As these emigrants took an active and honourable part in the transactions I am about to note, it may be proper to give some account of them, and of their country and character. They were descended from an ancient race of hardy, brave, and generous people. Some centuries previous to the emigration now spoken of, a quarrel had happened between two of their chieftains, respecting the possession of a woman, of great beauty, who had been taken and detained in one of their castles. Historians have disagreed as to some of the minor points in dispute; but all concur that the chieftain, who bore off the prize, had violated the rights of hospitality, and abused the confidence of his friend. This had drawn upon him the resentment of the neighbouring chiefs. To shield himself from the chastisement with which he was threatened, for his perfidy, he invited the emperor of Hindostan over to his aid. His majesty, being eager to seize upon every opportunity to extend his dominions, and not overly nice as to the means by which he should effect his object, hastened to the aid of the offending chief.

Having once gained footing on the island, he availed himself of the dissensions amongst the natives to protract his stay; and, under pretence of restoring the true and ancient worship of Brahma, and establishing an improved system of government, reduced them to a state of vassalage. In this state they have ever since been held by the Hindostans, but not without many bloody struggles to regain their native liberties.

It has been the policy of the Hindostans to keep the Boglanders in ignorance; and, as far as possible, to deny them every means of political and religious instruction. Discord has been excited amongst the several casts of society, and every attempt made by the natives to promote *"union,"* has been branded with the epithets of treason and rebellion.

But, notwithstanding all the oppressions heaped upon them, their noble spirit has never been broken. The historians of Hindostan have represented them as a ferocious and barbarous people, of great bodily strength, and sound constitution; but, withal, subject to a spasmodick affection, contracted by an unfortunate propensity, which they cherish, for tugging at a plant, found on the borders of their lakes, called CANAPE, and which is said to carry off great numbers of the natives every year. They are said to die in their shoes, cutting strange gambols with their feet in the air, to shew their contempt of death.*
Whether this be truth, or a slander invented by their

---

* It is true that the Boglanders often tug at the canape, but I am rather inclined to believe that, in proportion to their number, there are fewer canape tuggers in Bogland than in Hindostan.—*Thwackius.*

enemies, I shall not stop to inquire, but proceed to state, that in their native isle, they have few poisonous insects, and no "snakes in the grass."

The island being well adapted to grazing, they are said to succeed to admiration in rearing neat cattle, especially of the *male* kind. And it has been reported that, wherever the Boglanders have settled, or sojourned, in Hindostan or Saltatoria, *"horned cattle"* are to be found in abundance.

The Hindostanese generally represent the Boglander, as an ignorant, impudent, and turbulent animal.

So far as relates to the mass of the nation kept in ignorance by the jealous policy of their oppressors, there may be some truth in this representation; but it comes with an ill grace from those who labour to deprive them of the means of instruction.

A Boglander who has enjoyed the advantages of education, and breathed the air of freedom, is generally, a polite man, an active and enterprising citizen, a brave and honourable enemy, and an openhearted, candid, and munificent friend.*

---

* The testimony of all candid historians justifies me in giving this as the general character of the *educated* Boglanders. At the same time I am aware that, of late years, we have had some specimens of *"educated Boglanders,"* who merit all the reproaches cast upon their countrymen by their most violent enemies. These specimens, however, are generally, if not exclusively, from the deistical and atheistical schools of the muddle-pated Saltatorian philosophers.—*Thwackius.*

The Bogland emigrants, having felt the oppression of the emperor, in their native island, and fearing a visitation of it in their adopted country, joined heart and hand in every plan of defence proposed by the natives.

The people of Bawlfredonia had formed thin plates of horn, with so much elegance, that they transmitted light with wonderful beauty. They placed these plates in their windows. They were, also, becoming fond of painting, especially *caricatures;* and the Asylumonians, in their trading expeditions, had found a plant used in China, called herbata, which produced a broth of peculiarly stimulating qualities. This broth soon became a favourite beverage, and was generally introduced amongst the Bawlfredonians. The emperor resolved to put a stop to the importation and use of those articles in the colonies, by heavy imposts. He also hoped to make money, in the meantime, by the taxes; but *above all,* he wished to prevent the intromission of light by their windows; the use of paints, by which they sometimes exhibited wonderful caricatures of himself and his court; and the drinking of herbata broth, by which it was thought their prowess was increased, or rather produced.

If these measures prevailed, it was hoped that the people, deprived of light in their dwellings, of the means of caricaturing, and of their spirit, would become an easy prey to royal plans and officers. But it would not do. The Asylumonians were on the alert in all matters which had any concern with their interest, but especially their trade. They resolved to have light, paints, and herbata, at all hazards, except submission to royal impositions.

They would submit to no taxes on these or any other articles selected by the emperor, and were resolved to carry them in their own ships, and have nothing to do with those who traded on behalf of the king. The king's company of merchants had, in the meantime, brought a ship load of herbata, with a heavy duty upon it, paid into his coffers. Though the inhabitants were extravagantly fond of the herbata, and resolved not to be deprived of it, yet they would not suffer one pound of the taxed cargo to be landed. To crown the whole matter, the people of Puritanville rose, attacked the ship in the harbour, and threw the whole freight into the sea, with the most tremendous shouts of "herbata and no taxes," long live Bawlfredonian liberty!!!

No sooner did intelligence of these outrages, as they were called by the Hindostanese, reach the court of the emperor, than he swore ten thousand oaths that these things should not be. He issued a proclamation, prohibiting all intercourse with Puritanville, forbidding them to trade, and denouncing upon them the most appaling vengeance. An army was immediately embarked in the royal vessels of war, and conveyed to Puritanville, with orders to lay waste, by fire and sword, every part of Bawlfredonia that would manifest symptoms of rebellion. The emperor, in his rage, utterly forgot to advert to the well known character of the Bawlfredonians for prowess. By *"a sudden movement,"* the enemy took possession of Puritanville.

The Asylumonians, finding that their invaders had stolen a march upon them, were determined to keep a better look out in future, and, if possible, prevent them from extending their march into the country.

General Luparius, whose unbounded benevolence had gained him the affections of all to whom he was known, and whose great heroism commanded the confidence of his fellow-citizens, and inspired even the timid with courage, immediately sounded the alarm, and called his neighbours to arms.

Whilst their old men were engaged in writing letters, and despatching messengers to the interior of the colony for aid, every man in the parish, capable of bearing arms, followed their brave and intrepid general to the commons of Puritanville.

Knowing that their enemies were reported to be

a thieving set, and fearing that, by waiting until arms and ammunition could be procured from the publick magazine, they might have an opportunity of robbing the poultry yards, pig pens and onion patches in the neighbourhood, Luparius and his neighbours had not waited to supply themselves with any other weapons than their fowling-pieces and pitch-forks.

On their arrival, several eminences were pointed out to general Luparius, as eligible situations for encampment. Having been accustomed to encounter the wild beasts of the forest, in their dens and caverns, he was desirous to engage in *close action;* he, therefore, chose the hill nearest the town, where he could overlook the doings of the enemy, of whom thousands were engaged in devouring the poultry, onions and pumpkin-pies, of which they had plundered the citizens of Puritanville.

Luparius found that the number of the invaders was too great to justify his attacking them, until he should be supplied with a greater stock of powder and ball, and receive reinforcements, which were hourly expected. He was, however, resolved to interrupt their feasting. With this view, he applied to a brewer, on the bank of the river, and procured from him three-score of kegs, barrels, and tierces, which he threw into the water, a small distance above the town.

N

The Hindostanese, observing Luparius and some of his troops engaged on the margin of the river, and knowing his active and enterprising spirit, immediately concluded that he was contriving mischief against them.

No sooner, therefore, did they see the barrels and kegs approach the harbour, than they set up the most hideous shouts of "rebels! rebels! bloody rebels! Bawlfredonian rebels!" and instantly discharged at them all their great guns.

Some suspected that the kegs were charged with combustible matter, to blow up their ships, and deprive them of the means of escape, upon the arrival of the reinforcement which was expected by Luparius. Others swore, that the kegs were freighted with Bawlfredonians, packed up like pickled salmon, contriving, by this new mode of navigation, to pass down the river, and attack them in the rear.

An incessant firing upon the old kegs was kept up to the no small annoyance of the scaly tribe.

The fish that were wont to sport in the harbour, dived to the bottom, or fled out to sea; and not a porpoise dared to put his snout above water.*

---

* A poet of nature, from the half-way-house, who happened to be in Puritanville at that time, wrote a highly ludicrous and poetical account of this "*Battle of the beer barrels*," which was, on the same evening, set to musick, and sung by all the little boys on the streets, to the great mortification of the Hindostanese heroes. To this humorous song I am indebted for most of the facts relative to this great naval action.—*Thwackius.*

Great consternation pervaded the camp of the Hindostanese; and they would have been thrown into utter confusion, had not the address of captain Littlewood brought them to order.

Previous to the emperor's attempts upon the liberties of Bawlfredonia, this officer had obtained a furlough for the purpose of visiting some of his family connexions, who had emigrated to this country.

During his stay at Asylum Harbour, he became acquainted with general Luparius, and had accompanied him in several chases after the wild beasts of the forest, and in one or two expeditions against the savages.

In one of these expeditions, captain Littlewood, at the imminent risk of his life, saved a brave and respectable Asylumonian from the uplifted hatchet of the enemy.

Although greatly attached to the Asylumonians, his duty, as the king's soldier, imperiously called upon him to act against them.

Having heard that Luparius had been seen on the beach, and suspecting his object, he immediately ordered the firing to cease; and, mounting a gun-carriage, addressed the Hindostanese army to the following effect:—

"*Brother soldiers*,—In the absence of our general, I am called to address you. I regret that, without waiting for orders, so much powder has been wasted on the old kegs. Believe me, we have no time for trifling. The sentinels inform me that my old friend Luparius, commands the Bawlfredonian troops, and that he was this morning seen on the beach.

"I know this old soldier well, and can assure you that no enemy has hitherto found rest or safety in the neighbourhood of his camp.

"This launching of a fleet of kegs is only a trick to amuse us until he can obtain reinforcements. Wherever his flag is unfurled, he is sure to find adherents in plenty. We must, therefore, either proceed instantly to drive him from his position, or prepare to retrace our steps."

Towards the close of this address, general Modus, commander in chief of his majesty's forces, came rushing into the camp, half dressed, to learn the cause of the uproar.

Historians disagree as to the cause of the general's absence at the commencement of this memorable battle. All, however, concur that it was not cowardice which detained him. Some assert, that he was much given to gallantry, and that when the battle commenced, he was closely engaged, *tete a tete*, with the amorous wife of an old traitor, who had, on the previous evening, been despatched as a spy to

watch the movements of the Bawlfredonians. From
some intemperate expressions which fell from him
on the occasion, I am rather inclined to credit the assertion. Be that as it may, the cause of his distur-
bance put him into a most furious rage.

He swore, by all the gods in the heathen mytho-
logy, that the rebels should pay dear for their tricks.

"This old lion-catcher," said he, "has sent down
these kegs in order to send us a fool's errand after
them, while he should steal into town. They have
cost us some powder and shot:"—"And some sweat
too," said a fat corporal, who stood by. "He has"
*** a hiatus ***: "and by the insulted rites of
Venus he shall pay for it.

"I have been told that he is a most benevolent
man, and that he will, at any time, quit a tiger-hunt,
to assist a poor cottager in putting out a fire.

"Yonder lies a beautiful little village; let it be
instantly set on fire; and whilst the old codger and
his troops run to extinguish the flames, do you, my
brave soldiers, climb the hill, take him in the rear,
and we shall soon put him from playing any of his
Bawlfredonian tricks upon us."

In vain did captain Littlewood expostulate
against the folly and cruelty of this barbarous order:
the village was fired, and the poor peasants, with difficulty, rescued their wives and children, which were

the only articles they could save from destruction. But the object of the horrid act was not attained.

The Hindostanese soldiers, over eager in the work of destruction, fired the village in so many places, that, in an instant, it sent up a most tremendous blaze. Huge columns of fire and smoke, from every corner of the village, ascending to heaven, at once proclaimed the savage brutality of the foe, and convinced general Luparius that all attempts to save the property of the villagers would be in vain.

General Modus, finding that this *humane* expedient would not allure the Bawlfredonians from their position, resolved to drive them from it at the point of the bayonet.

For this purpose he ordered out ten companies of his broad-whiskered fencibles, twenty companies of light troops, and four companies of artillery. As the enemy advanced, general Luparius thus addressed his troops:—

"*My friends and fellow-soldiers,*—You see the dwellings of your neighbours in flames. Revenge their wrongs. Yonder come the authors of the mischief. We have no ammunition to throw away in random shooting.

"Remember how you have brought down the lions and tigers in the forest. Take good aim, and let no man fire until he is sure of his object."

The enemy had now advanced within thirty or forty paces, when a most deadly fire threw them into confusion, and caused them to retreat in disorder. Men of strong nerves, who had been accustomed to contend with the tigers of the forest, and to shooting off the heads of crows and black-birds, perched upon the tallest trees of the woods, could not well miss the heads, or the whiskers, of an enemy so near to them; of course every Bawlfredonian killed his man.

The Hindostan army being rallied by their remaining officers, and ashamed of having fled before less than half their number of *raw* troops, returned with firmness to the fight, but ere they could reach the brow of the hill, they were again thrown into confusion, by a fire equally destructive. With much difficulty, they were again urged to advance; captain Littlewood leading them on.

When he arrived within thirty or forty paces of the spot on which general Luparius stood, one of his young men pointed his fowling-piece at the captain. Littlewood saw him take aim, and had given himself up for dead, when he heard the voice of the general exclaiming, "For heaven's sake don't shoot that brave officer!—'twas he who slew Tecumhagano, and saved the life of your father!" The pointed gun instantly dropped; captain Littlewood bowed and retired. Such of his troops as survived the fire followed his example.

When the retiring troops reached the foot of the hill, they met general Modus with the whole of his army, and all his great guns from the ships in the harbour, advancing to their aid.

A fourth charge was made, and the camp of the Bawlfredonians was carried, at the expense of the lives of more than half the assailants.

The Bawlfredonians, after having expended their last shot, clubbed their fowling-pieces, and presented their pitch-forks, and did not retire until, by the aid of these weapons, they had filled their trenches with the dead bodies of their enemies.

General Luparius and his brave neighbours retired in good order to another eminence, a short distance from the town. In this situation he continued to watch the motion of the enemy, and cut off their foraging parties whenever they ventured out of reach of their great guns.

General Modus had no desire further to try the tug of war with "the old lion-catcher," but tamely suffered himself and his troops to be shut up in Puritanville, so long as the want of powder and great guns on the part of the Bawlfredonians, prevented their visiting his camp.

Amongst the Asylumonians, who marched to Puritanville, there was a man-midwife, called doctor Tincart. This fellow was such a prodigious boaster, that all his neighbours had predicted that he would run away at the first fire. In this, however, they were mistaken; he stood his ground during the battle, and marched off with his neighbours.

The doctor was excessively corpulent, and his waist was become so protuberant, that the wags of the town had circulated a report, that he himself would soon need the friendly aid of an accoucher.

Whether the doctor found himself too heavy for flight, or whether, upon this occasion, he mustered an uncommon stock of courage, is a point upon which historians are not agreed.

After the engagement, he kept a most prodigious bawling about the feats performed by him, *"in the day which tried men's courage."* He expected that, in the report of the battle, *honourable mention* would be made of his name. But, although all his neighbours had been astonished at finding that he did not run away, yet none of them had the charity to repeat his deeds of valour. Consequently, general Luparius suffered the doctor to remain the only trumpeter of his own fame.

This cruel neglect was severely felt by the doctor; but, as he was a prudent man, he took special care not to hint his displeasure to the general, nor did he say much about it until some thirty or forty years after the transaction, when general Luparius,

O

and most of his associates, were mouldering in their graves. Then, like a most valorous knight, he published to the world that GENERAL LUPARIUS WAS A COWARD!!! Nay, more—he asserted, most roundly, that the general was not in the battle at all; but that whilst he, the valiant doctor, and his neighbours, were fighting, *"blood to the knees,"* the general, regardless of the fray, was running about in the rear of the camp, picking up some old spades and mattocks, which had been thrown away by a company of ditchers, who had fled on the approach of the enemy.*

Having, for the present, *dismissed the doctor,* I proceed with pleasure to record the conduct of the good citizens of Blackmoreland toward their brethren in the north.

Upon hearing of the occurrences at Puritanville,

---

* Should I live to conclude this history, posterity will have cause to wonder at and admire the feats of this great doctor; who, by his profound skill in bawling, and stump oratory, raised himself to high eminence in the days of his friend king Tammany, to whom he was minister of war for three years, *"more or less."* In the reign of the most renowned king Pigman Puff, he was raised to the highest military honours, and would, no doubt, have immortalized his name by deeds of valour, had he not been visited with a most troublesome disease, which generally attacked him on the eve of a battle. This strange complaint occasioned a violent *shaking;* which, in spite of all medicine, *"uniformly increased as the moment of action approached."* The continuance of this unlucky disease caused his brother officers to recommend his removal to the hospital, from which he was not discharged until all the laurels, in the field of honour, had been gathered by his more fortunate brethren in arms.— *Thwackius.*

hundreds of the citizens of Blackmoreland hastened to the aid of their brethren, determined to share with them in all the difficulties and dangers of the war.

A general council, from every region of Bawlfredonia, was assembled at the half-way-house, between Puritanville and Nabobsburgh.

After a full consideration of the wrongs which they had suffered, it was resolved forthwith, to form a mighty army, and drive away every soldier of the emperor, out of the new world of the south, and have no further connexion with the parent state, as the Mogul empire was styled, than with any other of the Asiatic nations. A proclamation to that effect was issued; and every lover of liberty, independence and Bawlfredonia, was invited to repair, without delay, to the standard of his country, which was unfurled by the great national council.

The emperor heard of these bold measures with astonishment and dismay. His mind was greatly troubled, and he had even some thoughts of attempting an amicable adjustment of the differences; but a number of the nabobs, brahmins, and sycophants, who hoped to be advanced to great wealth and dignity in Bawlfredonia, excited and influenced his passions. He decreed to send over a great army, and a thousand ships of war. Before this could be accomplished much time was consumed. However, the army and the ships arrived in Bawlfredonia, burnt a great number of villages, and got possession of some large towns. Many wise people thought the whole country would be utterly destroyed.

It pleased heaven, however, to raise up a deliverer. The grand council appointed George Fredonius, descended in a direct line from the great and magnanimous discoverer of the country, to the chief command of their armies. He soon infused a vigour, and a spirit of order and subordination into the troops. He drove the enemy from Puritanville. * * * *

[Here follow several pages of this fragment, and two entire chapters relative to the war, written, as I understand from my friend O'Callaghan, by Monsieur Traducteur, under the pressure of a severe nervous complaint, with which he had been visited, and which occasioned a great tremour in his hand.—All the remaining numbers of the manuscript bear evident marks of this affection of the nerves of Monsieur Traducteur; and it is with the utmost labour I am able to decipher them. As I have a great aversion to labour in hot weather, and as the thermometer now stands at 98°, I shall, for the present, pass over a considerable portion of what remains, and forward to my publisher only such parts as can be most readily deciphered. Conscious of the effects of indolence, I dare not venture to make any promises to the publick. But I think it more than probable that, if my bookseller should not be ruined by his great liberality to poor authors, and his unbounded confidence in his friends, and thence be compelled to shut up his shop, I may hereafter favour the publick with what is at present omitted. But mark me, gentle reader, and you, my worthy bookseller, this must not be construed into a promise. My great, learned, and philosophick patron, whose profound researches into the secrets of the natural world, has so greatly enlightened this western hemisphere, and astonished the potentates of the north, may frown on my humble attempt to enrich his cabinet of wonders. The publick may become so much fatigued by reading the daily accounts of sea-serpents, two-headed bawling lizards, horned frogs, salt mountains, and prairie dogs, that they may be tempted to forswear books; or the Spaniards may kick up a dust in the south, or some one of a thousand other accidents may occur to induce me to throw by my pen, and forever decline the drudgery of translating. Having said thus much for myself, I proceed to Thwackius. But first, let the reader take his breath, and enjoy the cool air, if he can find any; and then, instead of censuring me for interrupting the narrative, extend his sympathy to a poor translator, labouring for the amusement and instruction of the world, in this hot month of July.—*Am. Trans.*]

*   *   *   *   *   *   *   *

It was the opinion of all the world, that heaven had fought for the Bawlfredonians. In fact, there could be no doubt of it; for on the day of the last decisive battle, angels were seen to hurl the thunderbolts of heaven upon the army of general, the nabob of Cornstalk.*   General George Fredonius was, however, the chief earthly instrument, and was, of course, deservedly *immortalized*, as we say.

*   *   *   *   *   *

* This I presume is merely a figurative manner of expressing, in oriental style, the aid of heaven.—*Fr. Trans.*

FRAGMENT IV.

During all these commotions, which I have now happily brought to a conclusion, the reader will, no doubt, be desirous to know how the people who had rejected the Christian religion, conducted themselves. Know then, that whilst old men and ministers of the gospel were shouldering their firelocks, and marching to the frontiers to protect their wives and children from the hatchet of the savage allies of the emperor, the members of the Bacchesian society *bawled* prodigiously, and fought little. One of them, a person of great distinction amongst these bold thinkers, made such a prodigious bawling in a small village of Blackmoreland, that a detachment of the invading army, passing within a mile of the village, mistook his noise for the braying of asses, and being in need of beasts of burthen, sent a corporal and three men to bring the asses.

As soon as the corporal made his appearance on the hill above the village, the bawler ordered his men, amounting to one hundred, to retreat. In the village he met with a provision cart, and jumping into it drove off full speed to a neighbouring mountain, and hid in a cave, where he remained several weeks, feeding upon some beef and bread which he found in the cart. The mountain was afterwards known by the name of *"Cart Mountain,"* from the vehicle in which he fled.

Upon the return of this bawler, whose name was Thomas Tammany Bawlfredonius, a descendant from Bawlfredonius, the pretended discoverer of our country, his friends expostulated with him on the subject of his shameful flight. He contended that no censure ought to be cast upon him on that account. Although he had fully adopted and admitted the opinion held by the society, that the soul and body were both composed of material substances, yet he alledged that they often acted in direct opposition to each other.

He asserted that his soul was brave, and panted for the fight, but that in spite of every opposition, his cowardly legs had carried him off the field of honour.

As it had often been asserted, that a red mantle inspired the wearer with courage, his friends advised that he should make trial of that colour, and that the remedy, to be more effectual, should be applied to the seat of the disease.

This advice was immediately followed. Thomas Tammany Bawlfredonius covered his legs and posteriors with red, and forever afterwards wore pantaloons of that colour. But this expedient did not succeed, and no effort could bring him to face an enemy in the field.

The society finding that their great and philosophical advocate could not be manufactured into *a man of war*, resolved that he should, at all hazards, be puffed into the character of a profound statesman. They reminded their fellow-citizens, that when nature denies an animal *one* faculty, she is sure to bestow upon him some other in an eminent degree; and, hence they concluded, that as their friend Tammany was no hero, he must, according to the immutable laws of nature, be a most accomplished statesman.

At one period a bold attempt was made by the Bacchesian society to deprive general Fredonius of the command of the Bawlfredonian army, and elevate, in his stead, an atheistical Hindostanese general, of the name of PHILO CANIS.

This general had seen some service in his native country, and had been hired out to one of the princes in the north, to aid in cutting the throats of some of his refractory neighbours.

In his manner he was rude, insolent, overbearing, and brutal. He had murdered his friend in a duel, and was of an immoral and impious character; he denied all divine revelation, and ridiculed religion, and religious men; and was, therefore, readily received as a worthy member of the society.

P

Having quarrelled with the emperor's officers before he left Hindostan, he abused them and the whole nation most heartily.

Our shallow-pated bawlers, mistaking this abuse, and his activity in persecuting the non-combatants, for patriotism, joined the Bacchesians in this attempt to promote their atheistical general. Fortunately, however, the good sense of the grand council defeated their machinations. Philo Canis retired from the army, irritated by disappointment, and soon after died of envy.

The Bacchesians were greatly mortified at the disappointment they met with in their attempts to promote their brother to the chief command. Some of them, however, continued in the service of their country, and fought like fiends until the Hindostanese were banished. But no sooner was the war ended, than the Bacchesian officers attempted to establish a military despotism in the land.

General Fredonius, by his great prudence and patriotism, soon put down this attempt. So completely did he expose the wickedness of their scheme, that none of the members dared openly to espouse the cause of their secret agents.

Jack Headstrong, then a subaltern in the army of Fredonius, was detected in attempting to excite a mutiny amongst the troops, by means of anonymous letters, written in the most artful and insidious style. The high respect which the general entertained for the brave, worthy, and pious father of the offender, induced him to spare his life.

Jack lived to see his brother Tammany on the throne, to enjoy the smiles and the favours of foreign courts, and to make a most conspicuous figure in the flight of our renowned king, Pigman Puff, and the destruction of his capital.

The Saltatorean officers had brought over with them their atheistical and deistical principle, and all the jargon of the new school.

Many of the young Bawlfredonian officers, who had been called from their parents, their schools, and colleges, before they had acquired a sufficient knowledge of revealed religion to enable them to withstand the attack of these infidels, were led astray by their sophistical arguments.

The Bacchesian society flourished greatly. Its meetings were still held in private. Thomas Tammany Bawlfredonius, who was early taken into the association, soon became the head of it. His plan was, to make their attacks upon religion all in the mining way. The ardour of Tom Anguish gave them no little trouble. However, a happy expedient was hit upon. He was employed to write pamphlets in favour of Bawlfredonian rights and independence, liberty and equality, herbata and no taxes, &c. and charged by the society not to give the smallest hint of his ultimate designs. When he had finished a pamphlet, it was laid before the society, and all the parts expunged which might lead to a disclosure of infidelity. By these pamphlets, which, indeed, contained many good things, said in a plain way, adapted to the lowest capacities, he acquired an amazing popularity. Even in Hindostan he was spoken of as dangerous to the repose of the empire.

As soon as the Bacchesian society found that he had written himself into reputation, it was decided, that his furious and infernal passion for open hostility, against all things held sacred and consecrated by the approbation of ages, should be indulged. He now bent all his powers, during the time he could spare from drunkenness and wenching, to the writing of a most daring attack on the holy scriptures. He gave it the title of "The Year of Philosophy." He denounced the whole Christian world as fools and idiots, or knaves and miscreants, and swore that no one had any pretensions to be considered a rational man, unless he rejected all religion, and indulged himself in the unrestrained gratification of his carnal appetite. That is to say, those who belonged to the Bacchesian society, and those only, were to be considered rational or reasonable beings!

The book, when read in the society, was saluted with such plaudits and acclamations, that the neighbours were roused from their deepest slumbers at the hour of midnight. Ben Shimei was instantly ordered to prepare an edition of twenty thousand copies at the expense of the society, and cause them to be distributed, gratis, through every region of Bawlfredonia. This order was executed with great zeal and expedition by this son of cursing; who, at the same time, issued a most furious philippick against the benevolent societies, which had been established for spreading the gospel among the heathen. Mr. T. T. Bawlfredonius caught that kind of inspiration which such a work was calculated to impart, and resolved, within himself, to write a book, which after much cogitation, he determined should assume the form of commentaries on the history of Blackmoreland. He was a true disciple of his brother Ophicus, of whom I have made honourable mention above; and, pursuant to his advice, resolved to fight under a mask. His book was soon finished. In it he affirmed that "it made no difference to him whether a man worshipped one God or fifty gods," provided he did not steal his venison, or take away his black Venus by force; that it was absurd to believe that the Almighty could make a general deluge so high as to cover the lofty

mountains of Bawlfredonia; for if he would condense
the whole atmosphere, it would not afford water
enough to raise the sea fifteen feet!!!—That the number of languages in Bawlfredonia, among the natives,
was so much greater than those of Asia, that no philosopher could question that the people of Bawlfredonia existed before those of Asia; that the native
Bawlfredonians could get more children in a given
time than men of civilized nations; (this he attempted
to prove by many philosophical particulars;) that they
were more excellent, and approached nearer to "perfectability" than civilized man; that a great natural
bridge in Blackmoreland had been actually built,
and nicely put together by a mere accidental convul-
sion of the earth; and, that it was absurd to suppose
that the Almighty had made it; that the sea had once
covered a great part of Bawlfredonia;—that—but why
need I add? Who after this can doubt that he was a
most profound philosopher?—Wonderful man! Thou
wert surely made to govern, and make nations happy!
Precisely so thought the society. As soon as his
commentaries were read, in solemn midnight convo-
cation of the Bacchesians, it was resolved to make
every effort to elevate him to the throne of Bawlfredonia, and in this they ultimately succeeded. But
before I relate the means to which they owed their
success, I must bring up the history of the newly
established commonwealth.

FRAGMENT V.

As soon as the independence of Bawlfredonia was secured, the grand desideratum was to form a system of government which might secure all the blessings likely to result from the new condition of things. Some were of opinion that Blackmoreland and Asylumonia should be entirely independent of each other. Indeed it was no easy matter to persuade the great body of Blackmorelanders to unite with the Asylumonians, for they were mortally afraid that these people would take their slaves from them by some trick, or some way interfere with their farming, or trading in stinkum-puff. At length, however, they agreed; and then the great difficulty was to fix upon the form of government. It was supposed by many that general George Fredonius might have made himself king, and the crown hereditary in his family. But he thought of no such matter. He wished to see the people permanently happy.

A great meeting of the delegates, from all parts of the country, was held at the half-way-house before mentioned, to form articles of a league, and establish a form of government by which the whole of the settlements of Bawlfredonia might be governed as one.

Now it was that the Bacchesian society, which had become exceedingly powerful, set all its machinery to work. It was feared exceedingly, lest some article might slip into the fundamental rules of government, by which the enemies of religion might be shut out from having any part in the management of governmental affairs. In fact, had it not been for the activity of the society and its agents, this would actually have happened. They raised a most prodigious hue and cry about the tyranny of the emperor of Hindostan in matters of religion, and stunned the ears of the whole country with their bawling about his persecutions. It was, indeed, true he had persecuted the best people in his empire for their religion, and so had all the other emperors, and nearly all the petty princes of Asia.

The society, in fact, knew very well, however, that in Bawlfredonia there was no danger to be apprehended from this quarter, where the people were remarkable for their uncommon liberality in all things relating to religion. But the fear of the society, and its agents, was, that open and avowed blasphemers, such as Mr. Thomas Anguish, would be excluded from the legislative council, and from the throne of the kingdom.

A delegate from Asylum Harbour insisted, that in the fundamental articles of the government, the

Almighty should be acknowledged as the supreme governor of nations, and his revealed will taken as a standard of civil and political morals.

"The Almighty," said he, "has protected us from our first settlement among the savages of the wilderness, has fought our battles, and almost miraculously made us a great and independent nation; and shall we now attempt to turn him out of the doors of the nation? The storms by which he destroyed the fleets of our enemies, the visible interposition of his arm, in many instances, during the conflict, but especially in the last decisive battle, call for a grateful acknowledgment at our hands. Besides, was it ever heard that a nation settled a form of government without the least mention of heaven, or recognition of its authority? Never. Our very aborigines do recognise heaven, or some invisible power. And shall we, who fled for the sake of our religion, do less?—I trust not.

"But further, we must have some clause: I say *must*, for I consider what I am about to say as absolutely essential to our national prosperity, not to say existence. We must have a clause, excluding those who belong to the sect of *Ahramanites*,* from places

* Ahraman was the name by which the principle of evil in the universe was called. He is worshipped by the savages that he may not inflict evil upon them. Some who belonged to the Bacchesian society, were hardy enough to broach, on occasions, their opinions among Christians, and

Q

of power and trust in the nation. It is well known that many of that sect deny a future state of rewards and punishments, and some, even the existence of God Almighty. Now, as we deem an oath necessary, as a security against the violation of the instrument we are framing, how will this oath bind the consciences of our Ahramanites? Again, I wish to see all openly impious, profane men, excluded from our legislative council, and the throne of the kingdom: Are not those publick functionaries set up as the guardians of national and individual morality. How farcical will it be to set up the most impious men in Bawlfredonia to prevent the people from becoming immoral? Leave the path of preferment open to them and they will soon jostle out of it all good men. Close the door upon them forever:—Yes, forever.

"Further, I wish to see the importation of black slaves entirely checked by an article in the fundamental laws of the kingdom; and, if possible, freedom granted to all who are among us." At this part of his speech the speaker was hissed. It was, however, the conclusion; and a severe rebuke from general Fredonius, who presided at the meeting, having

were called Ahramanites, chiefly from their not worshipping God Almighty, and laughing at those who did. It was hence supposed that they paid their worship to Ahraman alone; for it was thought impossible that a human being should live without any kind of worship.— *French Trans.*

produced an apology from the offenders, the member proceeded to read articles embracing the several points mentioned in his speech.

Most of the delegates were men of great talents and patriotism. Some, however, were Ahramanites, and members of the Bacchesian society. These Bacchesians, fearing the effects produced by the speech just delivered, proposed and obtained an adjournment until the next day.

In the course of the evening they held a meeting, to which they invited all whom they suspected to be tinctured with the new philosophy of the Saltatorean school.

In this meeting, one of the Bacchesians addressed his brethren to the following effect:—

"*My enlightened and philosophical brethren:*— The present crisis calls loudly and emphatically for the united exertions of every philosopher, and of every friend to the '*dignity of human nature.*'

"If the propositions made by this unenlightened, unphilosophical, and uncourtly onion planter shall prevail, in vain has the great Gibbonza written, and the immortal Humago reasoned.

"All our efforts to illuminate the human mind, and set free the consciences of men will become vain. We must either become a sober, plodding, praying and believing race, or be forever excluded from all places of honour and profit in the kingdom.

"To acknowledge the Almighty in our fundamental laws, would be most unphilosophically 'mixing
the affairs of church and state together.'   What! acknowledge, name the Almighty in a civil instrument
in Bawlfredonia! Preposterous!—Exclude from our
national councils and the throne of state, our greatest
and most profound politicians and philosophers, because they may happen to deny the existence of a
God, or a future state of rewards and punishments!
Horrible persecution!   Our country would soon be
a Talmunah, a field of blood!   Gracious heaven!
recognise the Bible, as containing laws of heaven
to be adopted in Bawlfredonia, a land of perfect
freedom! No.   And then, if a gentleman should happen to get drunk, or be guilty of some trifling impiety, bar the door against his entrance into the offices
and honours of the land, no matter how mighty his
talents! Again I say, forbid it the genius of liberty!
As to the oath, I see a slight inconsistency.   I wish
to see the oath banished.   To compel any one to
take it before he sits down in the national council, or
the throne of state, is downright persecution, and
mixing, most profanely, civil and religious affairs
together: things which differ *toto cœlo:* are even hostile to each other in many points!   No:—Let not that
stupendous fabrick of freedom, of which we are laying the foundation, whose top shall reach beyond the

stars, be deformed by any mention of religion, or the Almighty. Let the Ahramanite have the same privilege as any other citizen to sway the sceptre over those vast realms of Bawlfredonia, where every human being shall possess immaculate freedom!

"At the mention of the abolition of the importation of black slaves, my blood boils with rage. What! prevent us from importing and eternally enslaving these *soulless* animals? Make them free? But hold, admit they have souls, they have no right to be free. They had the abominable wickedness to be born black; yes, as black as a newly varnished boot. Make them free? Gross outrage upon our *"imperscriptible,"* imperishable, and natural rights. No: I invoke the genius of liberty to preserve to his Blackmorelanders the right of doing as we please. My fellow-delegates, what would our young sons, who are now growing up, and very near manhood *** hiatus ***: all already employed by those who have arrived at manhood, and the deficiency made by whipping to death, &c. must be supplied from abroad. If we are prohibited from importation, our stock will soon fail, and we shall—yes, we who are of nabob blood, shall be compelled to dig with our own hands in the soil, like the vulgar blood of the north. If we are encroached upon here, we shall utterly break off.—We end the league."

This speech was received with great applause; and after a free interchange of opinions amongst these free-thinking members, it was resolved, that they should stand by each other in resisting every attempt which the majority of the meeting then present, should deem likely to interfere with *"the sum of human happiness,"* or to check *"the march of the soul of man to perfectibility."*

The orator of the evening, then proposed that a full expression of the sentiments of the meeting should be made in the following resolutions:—

1st. That religion means any thing or nothing, and is altogether unnecessary to the prosperity of a nation. Therefore, to require of any freeman to acknowledge the Almighty, or to profess obedience to his revealed will, would be an unjust and tyrannical interference with the rights of self-government, at present happily enjoyed by all Bawlfredonians.

2d. That although we admit that all men are born equally free, that liberty is an inalienable and indefeisible right, yet we hold that to retain in slavery the "two-legged, unfeathered, black animals," now in possession of the citizens of Blackmoreland, is one of the indefeisible rights of freemen, and must be forever held sacred.

3d. That stinkum-puff is one of the luxuries of life, which no freeman ought to resign; and that the right to "grow it," trade in it, and enjoy it, must be guaranteed in the fundamental laws of the empire.

4th. That we pledge to each other our lives and sacred honours, to support these resolutions, and we engage not to vote for any article in the proposed constitution, by which any one of the principles above asserted, may be endangered.

These resolutions were no sooner read than adopted by a large majority. Some of the members present, who had not been admitted into the Bacchesian society, and who had still some qualms of conscience upon the score of religion, were somewhat startled at the bold avowal which they contained. But, having previously agreed that they would be bound by the decision of the majority of the meeting, to which they had been *politely invited,* they held themselves pledged to support the resolutions, by their votes on all questions agitated in the meeting of the delegates.

By this most artful contrivance the Bacchesians secured the votes of many, who, if left to the free exercise of their own judgment, would have voted for acknowledging the Almighty, and prohibiting the traffick in human flesh, and the growing of stinkum-puff.

When the delegates met, the Bacchesian members commenced the discussion; in which they expatiated largely on the great dangers to be apprehended from permitting any, the most remote connection, between civil and religious matters.

They recounted all the villanies practised by hypocritical priests, fanaticks, and pretenders to religion, and contended that as tyrants and hypocrites had practised fraud and persecution under pretence of religion, therefore, no wise politician ought to have any thing to do with it, but leave the matter wholly to old women, children, and priests.

Every Bacchesian being desirous to display his talents, in opposition to the proposition of the northern delegate, and most of them being very *"lengthy"* and very windy orators, they occupied much time, and made a most outrageous noise.

Their vociferous eloquence attracted great crowds around the hall. The whole day was taken up by the Bacchesians, who contrived to keep uninterrupted possession of the floor. Many of the lookers on were too indolent to think for themselves, and readily adopted, without examination, the sophistical arguments, and enormous conclusions of the orators. The delegates having adjourned without deciding the question, they had no sooner left their seats, than a most outrageous clamour was excited in the streets. The members of the Bacchesian society every where reported, that the northern fanaticks, as they termed

the Asylumonians, were attempting to insert a clause
in the constitution, to destroy all liberty of conscience.

It was said, that they intended to exclude from
office, all who eat eggs at Easter, or plumb-pudding
or mince-pies at Christmas, or who should refuse to
eat bacon on Fridays, or to aid in hanging witches.

The populace were completely frenzied and became tumultuous. Placards were set up at every
corner of the hall, on which appeared, in large letters, "LIBERTY OF CONSCIENCE:" "Beware of hypocrisy and priestcraft!!!"

At the next meeting of the delegates, general
Fredonius, and several others of the most respectable and intelligent members, advocated the rights of
heaven; and advanced such arguments in favour of
the recognition of the Almighty, as it was supposed
none could be hardy enough to deny. But all arguments were in vain; the Bacchesians were firm to
their purpose, and the weak and temporising delegates feared to oppose them. To be short--the point
was carried against heaven. The right of holding
black slaves, and growing stinkum-puff, were solemnly recognised.--The Bacchesians were trium-
phant.

As soon as the delegates separated, the fundamental laws were exhibited for publick inspection,
and adopted both in Blackmoreland and Asylumo-

R

nia; although the name of the Almighty was not once mentioned, nor any other standard of morals adopted than those of human invention. Many good people, when they had time to bethink themselves, were greatly alarmed; and predicted that, before forty years, heaven would send upon the country, pestilence, earthquakes and war.

But what did the Bacchesian society upon this occasion? Mr. Thomas Tammany Bawlfredonius, president of the society, got up a meeting of his neighbours, many of whom were pious people and abhorred the Ahramanites. It was not generally known that Mr. Bawlfredonius was an Ahramanite. He mounted a stump. Here let me pause, and describe the person of Thomas Tammany Bawlfredonius, and his appearance, as he stood upon the stump, in the midst of the gaping multitude:—He was six feet four inches high, and very slender. His legs were small, and without the gastroenimius muscles, *i. e.* without the calves. His knee-joints were large and close together, while his feet were ten inches apart. His shoulders were very large and high, extending nearly up to his ears. His chin hung far down the lower end of his lean face: while great quantities of loose skin overhung the corners of his mouth. His forehead was low; and his eyes, set in deep sockets, were generally half shut—a cer-

tain mark of great cunning. At his back, close by
the stump, was standing his Bacchesian brother Ahramanite, and most intimate bosom friend, Mr. Thomas Anguish. This gentleman was a stoop-shoul-
dered, carbuncle-faced, dull-looking, slender man.
He was to act the second part. As his book of Ahraman principles was not yet published, his genuine
character was not known. With this Mr. Anguish
for prompter, Bawlfredonius commenced his speech;
raising his long slender arm, the bones of which rat-
tled at every motion, above his head, and letting it
down, with violence, like the saw of a saw-mill.
This motion, in the graceful line of sawing beauty,
he continued to the end of his speech, which was to
the following effect:—

"*My dear fellow-citizens:*—I most gladly con-
gratulate you on the adoption of the fundamental
laws of the great kingdom of United Bawlfredonia.
All has been done that the most liberal mind could
wish, for securing the rights of every man. You
may, perhaps, feel some surprise that there has been
no mention made of the name of the Almighty. It
was not thought proper to profane that great name
by inserting it in a secular instrument. Neither has
that good system of morality, usually called the
Holy Bible, been alluded to, from the same pious
motive. It has, also, been thought probable that

this good book has suffered by careless transcribers; and, therefore, it was not thought best to bind the whole of it on the consciences of the deep philosophers; who, we hope, are to form our leading statesmen. On this delicate point, I express no opinion. That there might not be the least shew of persecution, or illiberality, no moral qualifications have been required as prerequisites in our legislators and kings. But as they are to be elected by the people, who in this enlightened kingdom cannot err, you will choose the good only to rule you. Our slaves, and the holy privilege of importing more, to enlighten them, have been solemnly guaranteed to the Blackmorelanders.

"I am indeed an enemy, in principle, to this involuntary slavery; but, as a right to this species of traffick, and property, has been established by the supreme law of the land, no one can, on solid grounds, object to it. I will also add, that we, of Blackmoreland, being the oldest colony, and having the greatest portion of political wisdom, and more morality, though less hypocrisy than the Asylumonians, ought to govern the empire of Bawlfredonia:—that is, we ought to furnish all the kings. Our grand destinies will henceforth develope themselves so as to fill the universe with admiration, at the political wisdom of the Blackmorelandean name.

"We ought to choose the wisest and most distinguished of our citizens, for promotion to the first dig-
nities of the empire. I shall not say who is the
most fit for our purpose."—"Yourself," exclaimed
Mr. Anguish:—"Yourself," re-echoed the multitude.
He went on:—"I receive, fellow citizens, your applause, as the earnest of future favours. For the
present, I hear the general sense of the nation is in
favour of our worthy citizen, general George Fredonius, who is certainly a gentleman of considerable
worth: though there may be some minor blemishes
in his character; I am disposed to conceal them, and
support him, especially as he is from Blackmoreland." Plaudite cives. The assembly was dissol-
ved with tumultuous acclamations.

On the same evening, the Bacchesian society had
a meeting, which was unusually full. At this meeting, a new edition of Tom Anguish's book, entitled
"The Year of Philosophy." was ordered to be printed with all convenient speed, and a subscription taken to defray the expenses. It was also resolved to
print, by order of the society, and by appropriations
from its exchequer, all books in favour of the sect of
the Abramanites. For then it was decreed that
Mr. Thomas Tammany Bawlfredonius, the worthy
president and supreme patron of the Abramanites,
should be elevated to the throne of the kingdom, as

soon as general Fredonius's term should expire.
The term appointed was twelve years. Here was
great foresight.

The immortal general Fredonius was unanimous-
ly elected king for twelve years. A grand council
was chosen, agreeably to the fundamental laws of
the empire, to legislate for the nation. And such
was the popularity of Thomas Tammany Bawlfredonius, in Blackmoreland, that king Fredonius
deemed it prulent to place him among his counsellors. For this he has been blamed, I think unjust-
ly. It is certain he did not know his Ahramanite
principles, or his ************. As I forgot to
mention it in the proper place, I am under the neces-
sity of stating, in further illustration of the character of this counsellor of state, now when we have
him elevated to the very footstool of the throne, that
his society maintained, that men were originally tadpoles; who, having cast their tails, are now making a
rapid march to perfectability—that all vegetables,
from the proud and lofty oak of the forest, to the
humble osier, and modest touch me-not, possess the
power of volition, reason, moral perception and sen-
sation; and are endowed with the faculty of encreas-
ing the circle of their felicities, by the delights of the
most refined connubial love—that the great continent
of Bawlfredonia was not formed by the Almighty,

but by a fortuitous conglomeration of sands pushed together by winds and tides—that a man might have as many wives as he could keep, provided the majority of them were black—that Ahraman made the Bible and ordained all the priests. Oh adventurous philosophy! How bold are thy flights into the ethereal regions of the most boundless——nonsense.

Here I might proceed to draw a picture of the empire of Bawlfredonia under the reign of the great and good Fredonius. But I should fall so far short of the original that I must not attempt it. I shall only say, agriculture poured its treasures in richest profusion into the lap of the farmer. The products of every land was borne on the wings of commerce into the marts of Bawlfredonia, and diffused through every limb of the empire. The arts of peace were cultivated. The song of the reaper was heard on the hills, and the lowing of cattle in the vales. Churches rose, and temples of science were erected, where the muses loved to haunt.

A central spot was selected by Fredonius, and a great city founded; and, by the grand council of the nation, called in honour of king Fredonius. Its site was near the northern part of Blackmoreland. Two splendid palaces were built; one for the king, the other for the grand council. After effecting all these objects, and resuscitating the credit of the nation.

which had sunk during the war, and a prosperous reign of eight years, he resigned his sceptre into the hands of the people; and his withdrawal into the bosom of his friends, in private life, was followed by the blessings of thousands and millions. Though with pain I record it, the Bacchesian society, or as they are generally called, the Ahramanites, towards the latter part of the reign of Fredonius, took prodigious pains to degrade him, with a view to advance Bawlfredonius; but only one depraved wretch, Ben Shemei, before mentioned, ventured openly to exult on his retiring from the throne. This fellow had been disappointed in his application for an office, and from the day of his disappointment, until the day of his death, he never ceased to utter railing and cursing against general Fredonius, and all his counsellors.

[The residue of this number, containing amongst other important matters, an account of the successor of Ben Shemei, and the part which he acted under subsequent monarchs, must be omitted for the present, for the same reasons which I have assigned for former omissions.—*American Trans.*]

FRAGMENT VI.

Before we dismiss the reign of Fredonius, it may be proper to take some notice of the most conspicuous characters who figured in his council.

[Here follow many pages of the most interesting biography, and the most profound political discussion, which, I hope, will not be lost to posterity; but for reasons already assigned, I cannot proceed further with the translation of them at present, than to lay before my readers what relates to an important little man, who, in after times, swayed the sceptre of the empire.] *Am. Trans.*

Mr. Pigman Puff was a remarkable nice little fellow, who wore rufled shirts and nicely blacked shoes on his pretty little feet, with all other articles of dress, as neat and spruce as a dancing-master from Saltatoria. His father and mother were plain people, living near the mountains in Blackmoreland, on a snug farm. They also were Christians of the strictest sect, called Elderites. Their son Pigman, when very young, was put to school, where he made great progress. As the best of schools were in Asylumonia, he was sent to one called Prince of Naskaw College, to complete his educa-

S

tion. There he commenced the study of divinity, to prepare himself for the office of a preacher, for which he was designed, both by himself and his parents. They had a society for prayer, where he prayed with great apparent earnestness. When he returned to his father's family, he became acquainted with Mr. Thomas Tammany Bawlfredonius, who was a lawyer, of some distinction, in the neighbourhood. Mr. Tammany discovered that Master Pigman was an active little fellow, who might be of use to him. He courted him, invited him to his house, and gave him some Ahramanite books to read. After all these preliminaries, he says to him, one day:—"Well, Pigman, I understand you are studying what they call divinity, that you are designed for a priest, and that you even begin to pray in publick. I am surprised, that a young gentleman of your promise, should not have acquired more liberal views. What! coop you up in a pulpit! How can you think of such an humble course?" Poor Pigman, truly, was very much dashed. He had heard religion so much sneered at, in the society which frequented the house of Mr. Tammany, that he began to be a little ashamed of it. Such an onset as this, before company, quite put him to the blush. After much hesitation, he made out to reply in the following words:—"Mr. Bawlfredonius, you will excuse

me if I say. that the pursuit you mention, in my opinion, is not so ignoble as is sometimes represented;
however, I have not thought of it. As to the story
of praying, it is not correct." Finally, young Puff
laid aside all thoughts of the pulpit, and commenced
the study of law, under the care of Mr. Tammany;
in whose house he was introduced to Mr. Thomas
Anguish, and was secretly initiated into the Bacchesian society, though he had still some compunctions
about the course he had taken.

Soon after he commenced the practice of the law,
he paid a visit to Asiaticksburgh, a great town, the
capital of Quakerania, which had increased with
wonderful rapidity. There, in a publick company,
he espoused the cause of Ahramanism, with all the
warmth and impudence of an inexperienced young
man. A proof that he had acquired sufficient impudence in the house of Bawlfredonius.

When this came to the ears of his pious father
and mother, their hearts were wrung with the bitter-
est agonies, as they, very justly, considered their
son ruined. They called him to severe account immediately on his return.

He had, however, learned the art of his preceptor. "Dear parents," said he, "I am as great an
enemy to Ahramanism as you can be. It is true, I

stated the arguments of the sect, as you heard, but it was with a view to have them refuted by Christian gentlemen who were present." So they were satisfied. Bawlfredonius also reproved him for his imprudence, and he became more cautious for the future.

Mr. Pigman was one of the delegates from Blackmoreland, for framing the fundamental laws of the nation; and took an active part in bringing about the union between Blackmoreland and Asylumonia.

During the sitting of the delegates, he renewed his acquaintance with many of his old fellow students at Naskaw college; and united with Alexander of New Frogland, and John Joddi, in a publication entitled, "The Unionist," in which the policy of the union, and the laws agreed upon by the delegates, were most ably defended.

Although Pigman had but a small share in this work: and although, on its first appearance, his Bacchesian friends abused it most heartily, yet, in process of time, they did not hesitate to quote this book as an evidence of his political wisdom and great literary talents.

Pigman was also a member of the first grand council, which met under Fredonius.

The most able and conspicuous members from Asylumonia, considered it good policy to conciliate the affections of the Blackmorelanders. With this view, great attention was paid to Mr. Pigman.

When any important measure was about to be introduced by the Asylumoneans, it was the practice of Alexander the cofferer, Roger Shearwood, Protector Lamedsworth, John Joddi, and may others of their most respectable colleagues, to furnish little Pigman with their notes and arguments, in favour of it, and to procure him to move and advocate it in the council.

By the aid of such able prompters, Mr. Pigman, for a time, shone most brilliantly in borrowed feathers. But grown vain of his popularity, and being much flattered and courted by his Bacchesian associates, he at length spurned the instructions of the Asylumonean counsellors. In direct opposition to their advice, he drew up, and proposed in the grand council of the nation, a new set of commercial regulations, and introduced many other most absurd and preposterous measures, highly injurious to the interests of the state.

The Asylumoneans exposed the folly and absurdity of his silly projects. His pride was mortified; and his Bacchesian flatterers urged him to an open breach with his old instructors. From that period, until the day of his death, he was the most decided and malignant enemy of the Asylumoneans.*

* * * * * * * * *

* When Heaven, in vengeance for our sins, permitted this little man to ascend the throne, and plunge our country, unprepared, into a most bloody war, he withdrew the national troops from the defence of Asylumonia. When the prowess of our citizens had convinced our enemy, "that we could conquer, though our king should fly," Pigman patched up a treaty of peace, in which he "remembered to forget" to secure to the fishermen of Asylumonia, the privileges which had been guaranteed to them by all former treaties. So far will wounded pride carry a little soul! But of this, more hereafter.—*Thwackius.*

FRAGMENT VII.

About this period there was a most tremendous caper cut, by the great empire of Saltatoria, east of Hindostan.

The Saltatoreans were a strange heterogeneous mass. They had, amongst them, some learned and pious men, and many great warriors; but the greater portion of their population was composed of a thoughtless, fiddling, dancing, singing, and capering people.

The country was, at the same time, overrun by herds of vain, impudent, and superficial pretenders to philosophy; who were constantly ergaged in publishing, amongst the most ignorant of the people, what they termed new and important discoveries in the sciences of jurisprudence, and moral and political philosophy. They asserted, that there was nothing in the universe superior to human reason, tutored by modern philosophy. That as soon as the human family could have this omnipotent reason enlightened and schooled by their divine philosophy, the golden age would be restored. There would no longer be occasion, either for parental authority, or

for framing or enforcing penal laws. They asserted that, inasmuch as "men were begotten and
brought into the world for the mere pleasure of
their parents, and without their own consent, all
exercise of parental or legislative authority was
downright usurpation and tyranny." That as soon
as these principles should be universally acknowledged, all coercion should cease; but that, in the
mean time, it was expedient for them to hasten the
perfectibility of man, by cutting off the heads, and
seizing the property of all who should oppose their
benevolent doctrines.

These sophists, although they often disagreed
upon minor points, all united in deriding every thing
held sacred by their ancestors. They spared no
pains to gain proselytes, and their success was full
as great as Ahraman, himself, could have wished.
The government, under which they lived, was a
despotism. The reigning tyrant was more mild
and humane than most of his predecessors; and,
whatever other vices he had, it was evident that he
greatly disliked the shedding of blood. His for-
bearance encouraged the sophists to publish their
opinions without reserve.

Some of his young officers had been in Bawlfredonia during the war, and had fought under Fredonius. They believed, when they returned home,

that they could enjoy freedom as well as the Bawl-fredonians.—Huge blunder!!—They went to work, aided by the sophist—slew the emperor, his wife and children, and granted a commission to a butcher and a mountebank, to put to death all who should by word or deed oppose their new doctrines. These officers of reformation raised a powerful army, took the heads off fifty thousand priests and nobles, and cut the throats of five hundred thousand men women and children. But what above all things delighted the Ahramanites of Bowlfredonia, was, that these reformers swore most stoutly that the Bible was imposed upon the world by a trick of Ahraman, and that none but fools could believe in a God, or a future state of existence, or worship any deity except Venus and her *yielding* nymphs.

As soon as this news reached Bawlfredonia, the Bacchesian society sent over Mr. Thomas Anguish to assist their Saltatorean brethren in the grand work of reformation.

There he made some figure, aided by the advice of doctor Philip Phlogiston, Peter Potasia, and some other Hindostanese embarked in the same voyage of experiment. His Bacchesian friends expected that he would be prefered to great honours under the new order of things in Saltatoria, but his brethren in one of their freaks, resolved to chop off his head and

T

dut it into doctor Phlogiston's crucible, in order to ascertain whether or not he had a soul. He however made his escape before his brethren had leisure to try the experiment, and conveyed intelligence of his danger to his friend Bawlfredonius, who immediately sent a ship to bring him off.

Doctor Phlogiston and his friend Potasia, finding the weather rather stormy in Saltatoria, soon returned to their native land. Some historians have affirmed that Phlogiston never shewed himself publickly in Saltatoria during their troubles, but that he trusted his lectures and his plans to his friend Potasia, who was a man of great courage, so great indeed was his temerity, that upon one occasion, he did not hesitate to take the Saltatorean butcher by the beard. Be that as it may, it is most certain, that they did not make much stay in Saltatoria. Nor were they long in their native country after their return.

Whilst in Hindostan, the doctor had made professions of what he called CHRISTIANITY; but the great body of Christians disclaimed him and all his new fangled doctrines, considering them as none other than the invention of Ahraman to sow divisions and heresies in the church, and promote the cause of Mahomet, with whom the Doctor and his friends had proposed an union.

With great professions of meekness and humani-

ty, the doctor was excessively vain and opiniated.
He asserted that he fully comprehended and could ra-
tionally explain and account for every phenomenon,
both in the natural and spiritual world, and that it was
altogether impossible for any thing above his compre-
hension, to have existence in either. He professed to
believe in divine revelation, yet declared that he
neither could, nor would believe any thing contrary
to his own ideas of order and propriety, although it
should be revealed to him in person by an angel from
heaven, and that in such case, he would tell the angel
to his teeth, that he was a lying spirit.

This modest gentleman did not hesitate to assert
that he was a much better casuist, a more learned
divine, and a more orthodox Christian than saint
Paul. He said, that Moses was at best, but an in-
accurate and *"lame"* historian. He also declared,
that rather than give up a favourite theory, or submit
his better judgment to the evidence of the apostle
John, "he would be willing to believe that the old
man had mistaken or forgotton the words of his
Master, or that Christ himself had spoken and acted
under a delusion!!!!"*

* However arrogant and impious such assertions may appear to the
reader, I can assure him that the Doctor had many disciples in Bawlfredonia. With considerable talents and acquirements in one science, and
by the most laborious research in many others, which he was incapable of
comprehending, he made a great figure at the head of a set of most su-

His friend Potasia belonged to the sect of Broscovian philosophers, who placed their supreme delight in eating and drinking, and asserted that the
Deity had formed all animal, rational and vegitable
creation, with equal faculties to discern and enjoy
the Supreme good. They also asserted, that it was
impossible to believe that the Supreme Being would
condescend to look after such a poor and contempti-
ble race, as the sons of Adam.

The doctor had some good qualities, and possessed great knowledge in alchymy. But he was so
fond of contradiction, and so anxious to be accounted
a universal genius, that he was led into innumerable
errours and absurdities, especially upon the subjects

perficial, vain and arrogant coxcombs, who having acquired some smat-
tering in foreign languages, employed themselves in ransacking the
musty manuscripts of old fools and hereticks, and dressing up their
strange and long exploded doctrines in a new garb. These men profess-
ing themselves masters of all science, inundated the world with their
books. They affected to treat with the utmost contempt all the philosophers of the old school, nor would they admit that any man had the least
pretensions to learning or common sense, unless he would give up all his
old opinions and profess implicit faith in their new fangled doctrines.
They greatly courted all pretenders to science. In their publications,
by the help of translation and by stealing from ancient authors, they contrived to copy out some accurate experiments in natural philosophy,
some self-evident maxims in moral science, or some other plain and
incontrovertible principles, familiar to the learned, but little attended to
by the illiterate.—With such evidence of learning, which they took care to
display before the illiterate, with all the pomp and ostentation of mount-
ebanks, they were enabled to pass amongst the little and the great vulgar, for men of profound wisdom and erudition and many an empty pate
was set agog by their multifarious scribbling.—*French Translator.*

of theology and politicks. It was shrewdly suspected that he, in common with his followers, was in the
habit of borrowing the discoveries of his neighbours,
and passing them off as his own; but for the truth of
this, I cannot vouch. His cotemporaries, however,
asserted that he and his friend Peter Potasia, having acquired considerable knowledge of foreign languages, and translating many of them with facility,
made free use of their translations in the lectures
which they delivered, and the numerous books on
Theology, Alchymy, Politicks and History, with
which they deluged the Hindostan empire.

The doctor attempting to astonish the world by
an analysis of a whirlwind, burst his bottles and re-
ceivers, and blew the roofs off half the houses in the
village, and sent many of the inhabitants to take *"a
long sleep."* His friend Potasia having invented a
new method of whitening gunpowder, in his first experiment on a large scale, blew up a magazine and
set fire to the village at the instant in which the inhabitants were engaged in renewing the roofs of their
dwellings.

These unlucky experiments drew down upon the
unfortunate philosophers, the resentment of the mob,
who burnt their laboratory and books, and compelled them to flee for safety to Bawlfredonia, the great
asylum of *"oppressed humanity."*

Now as the "gunpowder plot," and the alchymy of whirlwinds, supposed to have been produced by a "metallick currency," rather a scarce article, had not succeeded, the learned doctor Phlogiston, resolved to enter upon some omniferous chymical munifi- lutions in Balfredonia; a mere project of course. But as the good people of this enlightened commonwealth were fond of *experiments,* he was pretty certain of attracting the notice of some of our most conspicu- ous characters. Indeed before he entered upon his mysterious compositions and decompositions, the Bawlfredonian territory resounded with his name. Our Savins had heard of the explosion of the gun- powder, and the ravages of the exasperated whirl- wind. They said, though he and his friend Pota- sia had failed in their ultimate designs, in those un- dertakings, yet they had failed gloriously in a noble cause, and in a most intrepid experiment. For who had ever heard of analyzing a whirlwind? It is true there were some suspicions awake, that their only object had been to burst the bottles, and explode the gunpowder, that they might thereby blow up the strong holds of religion and government in the South of Asia. But as the Balfredonians are not naturally a suspicious people, those misgivings did not ope- rate much to the disadvantage of these adventurous philosophers.

Now gentle reader, and ye most sapient tribe of wonder working philosophers of the renouned Saltatorean school, what do you suppose should be the project of the great doctor Phlogiston? Why, truly he resolved by hook or by crook, to get the head of the king of Bawlfredonia into one of his crucibles for sublimation. But as the worthy old George Fredonius was then on the throne, who had too much age, good sense and experience, to put his head into any crucible, and more especially one made in Hindostan, nothing could be done in that way for the present. The doctor and his friends would occasionally broach some of his new fangled doctrines in the presence of Fredonius, but the sedate and dignified manners, and the sterling good sense of this august personage, never failed to put to silence the whole tribe of projectors.

The doctor utterly despairing of making any impressions upon king Fredonius, fixed upon one of the most aspiring lords of his household, John of Onionville, who had managed the national intercourse with the emperor and nabobs of Hindostan. The doctor was the more solicitous to carry his point with John of Onionville, as he thought he could perceive that he was destined soon to fill the throne.

He did not venture to propose the matter immediately, but recounted the exploits he had performed on whirlwinds, &c. to the very great astoundment of lord John, whose brain the doctor actually began to carry away in the whirlings of the wind, which issued from the front door of his pericraneum.

Amidst this whirling of his brain, John spoke amongst his Onionville friends with the most heated enthusiasm of the marvellous powers of the Hindostanese alchymist, little thinking, honest man, of the designs that were forming against his own head.

Amongst the many novel and wonderful theories started by this alchymical experimenter, he asserted that, "a philosopher should not believe any thing which he could not see and feel." As this however was the age of experiments, he taught this maxim with wonderful success, affirming that it was even an axiom, though he most stoutly denied, and so did his coadjutor, the cunning little chuffy Potasia, "that there are any first principles." They even affirmed that there was no such commodity in the great market place of the world as *common sense.* This was the more wonderful, as their magnus apollo, Tom Anguish, in his book called "The year of philosophy," has, as he alleged, treated this article most learnedly, and asserted that it was to be found in superabundence in this most enlightened nation.

They denied too, that there was any such beings

as Ahraman and his followers, at least they affirmed that they never took any part in the affairs of mortals.

This assertion at first, a little startled even the credulity of lord John, for he had been educated in a sober and sensible way, and had one time entertained some thoughts of becoming a preacher of Chistianity. He had heard it whispered by some plain people, that Ahraman had sent out a detachment of his infernal soldiery to guard the vessels that had brought over Phlogiston, Potasia, and Anguish to prosecute their labours in this land of liberty, and when he heard the doctrine of their existence so badly attacked, a thought passed over his *silla turcica* and through the pineal gland, where he thought his soul kept its head quarters, though his two learned alchymists said that he had no soul, and that there is no such article in the world; I say a thought passed through the head quarters of his soul, for I, Harman Thwackius, historian, &c. do believe in souls, that they had denied the existence of Ahraman, merely to silence the clamour that had been raised, of his sending a convoy with them across the Indian ocean. However, doctor Phlogiston assured him he could never get an Ahraman into his retorts, and he was certain, that had they existed, he would have found them there. This satisfied John.

U

While the whirlwind of these opinions was agitating the head of lord John, and had nearly blown the roof off his brains, he became very noisy among his friends in the north, and raised such an uproar in the pericraneums of his northern acquaintances that it was never quelled until of late, when many of the *revera* had their brains unroofed. For dull and dogmatical as lord John was, the people of Onionville, and a large portion of his northern neighbours, thought him a great man, and many of them believed all that he said. Hence doctor Phlogiston, the prime mover of all those vagaries, set every thing agog in the northern regions of Bawlfredonia.

This foreign philosopher at first proceeded with much caution, but finding that his opinions were eagerly swallowed, he no longer hesitated to avow his boldest theories, and declared his belief in the non-existence of the human soul, and the notion that man rots in toto, when he dies, like a log, which he said had as much common sense, when a living tree, as any man. Now as lord John had some vanity, he refused to admit this doctrine. The experiments, cucurbiet, retort and crucible were again resorted to, but here it was hard to gain his assent.

While this dispute was in the full tide of sucessful experiment, the venerable father of our country, the wise heroick and benevolent king Fredonius, announced his abdication of the throne. Lord John of Onionville, and Thomas Tammany Bawlfredonius were the only candidates for the crown.

John invented many cunning plans for securing his election. The orderly and pious part of the nation, who knew nothing of his new notions, which went to overturn all that they had ever believed, in philosophy and religion, generally took part with John, whilst the Ahramanites to a man sided with Tammany, who they knew to be a thorough going Bacchesian. John they considered as only a half way character. John out polled Thomas, and was of course crowned king. According to the fundamental laws of the kingdom, Thomas being the next highest in votes, was promoted to the second post of honour and power.—On their elvation, both played their parts perfectly in character.

John having been elevated by the votes of the Christians, and believing that in certain districts, it was necessary to keep up appearances, affected to treat the name of the Redeemer with holy veneration, notwithstanding his secret denial of his divinity. Indeed in one of his proclamations for a fast, he ven went so far as to invite the nation to pray in that sacred name, to the boundless laughter and scorn of the Ahramanites. They declared, that to invite the nation to pray in the Redeemers name, was a most offensive mixing of sacred and civil things together, and that the fasting of John was down right hypocrisy. In truth they called all religion by that name.

Thomas Tammany delivered a long speech to the national representatives, and caused it every where to be published, in which he asserted most roundly, that he never had the vanity to aspire to the crown, and that there was no man in the nation whom he would more cheerfully obey than the wise and great lord John of Onionville. Many of the simple ones belived him, whilst the better informed and more discerning men of the nation, weighed both these great men in the balance, and pronouced them wanting.

Often during the evervesence into which the brain of lord John was thrown by the near prospect of a crown, the doctor attempted to move the question of the souls nihility; but either because John thought a king should have a soul, or that it required a soul to gain a throne, which may be doubted, or rather that he had no time to attend to the business, he could not be induced to investigate the subtleties of his philosophical friend.

As soon however as he had got the crown fairly bound on his head, doctor Phlogiston modestly requested the king to be so good as just to let him put his head into the crucible, in order that he might analyze it, for the purpose of settling the long contested point, whether a man, a log and a cabbage head, belonged to the same genus, *i. e.* whether they be equally soulless.

The king at first stood aghast, astounded, astonished, dismayed and amazed at the proposition, thinking the doctor either mad, or a murderer sent over by the great mogul, to evaporate, in cucurbits, the heads of Bawlfredonia's kings. In truth, he was nearly petrified by such a proposal from one whom he had thought the prince of philosophers. At length, recovering from his sime-torpor, "Why doctor, doctor!—dear doctor Phlogiston, put my head in a crucible:—Analyze my head!!—Oh! I perceive now you were in jest."

Doctor Phlogiston maintaining the most solemn gravity, and philosophical sang-froid, replied, "King John, you surprize me. Are you not sensible that the question, whether a man is a rational creature, with an immortal soul, or only a mushroom, produced by the mere jumbling together of atoms, is a question of the greatest importance to philosophy? I wish to try the experiment on the brain of a king, just supposing that if he is found to have none, then the business will be brought to a happy issue. My Saltatorean friends wished to try the experiment upon that illiterate coxcomb, Tom Anguish; but he, like a fool, played them the slip, and had they even tried his muddled pate, it would not have decided the question; as it is asserted that he cannot be made of the same stuff with *men*, otherwise he would never have sold his wife so cheap. But an experiment upon you, my dear friend, would put the question beyond all doubt. Besides, my friend, the Broscovian, Peter Potasia, begins now to know something of alchymy, and I wish him to perform the operation under my direction. Don't wonder that I, who have attacked the god of Hindostan and Bawlfredonia, and all their religion, and have satisfied them of the non-existence of Ahraman, should think it a great matter to put the head of a king, which I hold to be a mere mushroom, into my crucible, that I and my friend Potasia might prove it to be such, and—" "Stop, stop! hold," said the king, in a fury, for he was a very passionate man, "You impudent Hindostan.—What! does the fellow mean to roast my head alive with my own consent!!!—"Thou art an emissary from Delhi!—Begone from my court, and had I the power, I would banish all the Phlogiston's and Potasia's from my empire."

The doctor, not in the least disconcerted, but supposing that when his passion was gone off, he could readily procure a reconciliation with the cholerick king, leisurely retired from his court.

The two philosophers fixed their residence in a beautiful little village on the banks of a grand river in the district of Quakerania, about half way between Nabobsburgh and Puritanville. Here they preached their doctrines with great success, the neighbourhood abounding in soft headed people, who seldom left their houses, but were very fond of news, and believed that all wisdom must come from afar.

Although doctor Phlogiston did not much relish sailing on the tempestuous ocean of liberty, he and his friend were both most ardently attached to the Saltatoreans. The doctor even asserted, that the tumults which shook their empire, were the first fruits and very beginning of a millenium of holiness and happiness which was to bless the world. King John on the contrary had a great hatred to the Saltatorians, and an insatiable desire to go to war with them, on account of their great insolence.

He also had an aversion to the Hindostanese, and greatly dreaded their rivalship in the trade of the east. To guard against the machinations of these powerful neighbours, he set about building ships of war, and raising a small army.

Bawlfredonius affected to believe, and he and his friends every where asserted, that these fleets and this army was designed by John to enslave the Bawlfredonians, turn the limited monarchy into an absolute despotism, and support ranks like the casts and nabobs of Hindostan. John had no such intention. But the story served as a pretext to further the views of the Bacchesians, in promoting their most active member to the throne of the empire.

In the midst of the uproar occasioned by these measures of king John and the slanders of his enemies, he resolved to send an ambassador to the emperour of Hindostan, to settle some old accounts between the nations, which had remained open from the time of their seperation. Doctor Phlogiston thinking that this embassy might afford a good job for his active and enterprising friend Potasia, and hoping that king John had forgotten the crucible, without much cerimony, wrote him a letter, request-him to appoint his friend ambassador; assuring him that Potasia was a most active negotiator and a good accountant. That he had an old quarrel with the emperour, and would not fail to fleece him in the settlement, unless his clerks had kept their accounts more accurate than usual.

When king John read this letter, he flew into a violent passion. He remembered the crucible, and feared that if he should renew his intercourse with the philosophers, another attempt might be made upon his brains. "Here is," said he "no limits to the impudence of these foreigners. What! have we not Bawlfredonians that we can intrust with the management of our affairs, without the interference of strangers? No, I shall not send Potasia, as my ambassador to Hindostan, I know nothing of him."

As soon as doctor Phlogiston, and Mr. Potasia, heard the fate of their application to king John, they vowed vengence, and took an open and decided part with the chiefs of the Bacchesian society, and wrote and circulated the most violent attacks on king John, and his whole party.

King John had been so often slandered with impunity, that his assailants took no pains to conceal their attacks. Potasia in order to shew his bravery, carried some of his libels to one of king John's officers, telling him that: "I, Peter Potasia, wrote this little book." The officer seized upon Potasia, and put him in custody, until he could inform the king of his offence and his impudent avowal of it.—King John, as a punishment for his impudence, ordered him to be shut up for thirty days in a cage, set opposite to a most restless, slavering and spitting Bogland lyon, which had been purchased shortly before that period, by an Onionville farmer, for a pair of bullocks.

Although Potasia had a great desire to cut a figure in the political world, and to pass for a persecuted patriot, he did not much relish his cage; being

W

neat in his person, and a gentleman, in his deport-
ment, he could not endure the spitting and slavering
of his beastly neighbour, or the rude familiarity of
the lower order of Bacchesians, who flocked in great
numbers to condole with him on his sufferings.

He was too much of a soldier to complain of the
punishment he had courted, but he insisted that
king John was a most partial ruler. That he punished foreigners for things which he permitted natives to do with impunity. He said that Alexander
the cofferer, of the district of New Frogland, had
written a most severe, a cutting satire, upon king
John, and swore most stoutly that he should be
punished, or there was an end to all fair play in
Bawlfredonia.

No sooner was Potasia released from his cage,
than he brushed up his beaver, fumigated his clothes,
and mounting a pacing nag, furnished by one of his
Bacchesian friends, set out for New Frogland.

Arrived at the house of the cofferer, and having
obtained admission in his drawing room, after
making one of his best bows, he thus addressed him:

"Fellow Citizen,

"My name is Potasia, I was born in
Hindostan, I did my native country some service,
and they know it. But they were unworthy of me,
and my great and learned friend Phlogiston.—I went

over to assist the Saltatorian patriots in regaining their
liberties, but their insolent butcher insulted me.—I
challenged him, he refused me the satisfaction due to
a gentleman, and I scorned to tarry in the dominions
of such a paltroon.—I visited your country.—I offered to devote my time and my talents to the service
of your king.—He spurned my offer, and treated me
with disdain.—I satirized him, and instead of meanly shrinking from danger, I avowed the act to his
officers.

"For this open, manly and candid conduct, I
have been shut up in a cage for the space of thirty
days, oppressed by the hateful sight of a most offensive beast, and a combination of all the villainous
smells upon earth.

"I understand that you have also satirized old
king John.—I call upon you as a man and a soldier,
to avow the fact, that I may know whether impar-
tial justice is administered in this boasted land of
"liberty and laws."

At the delivery of this speech, Alexander was
almost as much astonished as was old king John,
when Dr. Phlogiston proposed putting his head into
a crucible. But he took it in better part. In fact he
laughed most heartily at the proposition. "Thank
you, thank you, my friend," cried Alexander, "I am
not disposed to turn knight errant, I shall not willing-

ly run my head against a stone wall, or my body into your cage.—I regret that you have put yourself to the trouble of taking so long a journey on my account. If you will be pleased to quench your thirst and satisfy your appetite with what my side board affords, I will wish you a good journey back again."

Potasia, who when he took time to reflect, was not deficient in common sense, could not avoid laughing at his own folly, and availing himself of the polite offer of Alexander, he took a hearty swig of his favourite beverage, a stout luncheon of cold ham and white loaf, and mounting his nag, bent his course homeward.

I might have informed my reader sooner, that the people of the commonwealth of Bawlfredonia, by the fundamental laws of the kingdom, had the power to dethrone their kings by a general election, without chopping off their heads, as is the practice of most other nations.

No sooner was John seated in the car of state, than his hypocritical friend and elogist, Thomas Tammany Bawlfredonius, and his Ahramanite confederates, began to plot in secret, how they might dethrone him.

King John was guilty of some indiscretions. He was a most insufferable egotist, and was vastly proud of his acquirements in jurisprudence and theology.

His proud and haughty airs, caused him to quarrel with Alexander the cofferer, Timothy the scribe, and many others of the old and confidential counsellors of king Fredonius His vanity exposed him to the snares of the sophists.

His great hatred to the Saltatorian nation, and the circumstance of his having written a book on civil government, containing doctrines which were greatly reprobated by the Saltatorian constitution mongers, prevented him from adopting any of their new theories upon civil government. He was willing to admit that he had a soul to be saved. Yet he could not be brought to believe that it would be saved according to the old and received doctrine taught by saint Paul and the apostles, but, "By the deeds of the law," and by his own meritorious works. To a man "Wise in his own eyes," Christian humility is a lesson hard to be learned; and "pride goeth before a fall."

What greatly embittered the fall of John, was, that it was not for any of his evil deeds that he was put down. These caused his friends to mourn. But for his good works, upon which he so much depended, and for which he hoped to be rewarded, both in this life, and that which is to come; he was greatly persecuted by the Bacchesian society. His most meritorious conduct was grossly vilified, his most upright intention called in question, and every effort made by him, to secure the rights and liberties of our country, were represented as the most wicked machinations for enslaving and oppressing his subjects.

What effect these persecutions had upon his religious opinions, we are not explicitly informed, but from what I can learn of his conduct towards the close of life, I have reason to believe that he was brought to acknowledge, that "He who performs good works only, with a view to the applause of mankind, or in hopes of thereby meriting the joys of heaven, will find himself miserably disappointed, as well in this life, as that which is to come. When we have received credit for all our good actions, and come to be weighed in the balance, we shall be found wanting, and discover that without the efficacy of pardoning mercy, none of us can hope for salvation."

The Aramanites, amongst their other vices, indulged themselves in lying upon all occasions. and they never hesitated to invent and circulate the most impudent and bare faced falsehoods, to effect their purposes, especially when a throne was at stake. Whenever a state or electioneering lie was set afloat by Thomas Tammany, Pigman Puff, or any of the bellwethers of their faction; every district bawler, from one end of the kingdom to the other, was prepared to repeat the falsehood with loud vociferations. If any attempted to contradict the story, instantly the whole pack of Aramanites was let loose upon him, and he was cried down as an enemy to freedom, and a moral traitor. It was in vain to appeal to the most respectable testimony, or the plainest reason in contradiction of such falsehoods, however absurd. The former assertions and the contradictory statements, whether verbal or written, of Thomas Tammany, or Pigman Puff, were appealed to in vain. The maxim of the bawlers was, "A publick favourite can do no wrong." It therefore mattered not, whether such an one spoke falsehood or truth. It was enough for him to speak, and every member of the faction was bound to support the assertion, whether true or false, upon pain of expulsion. Many of the Bawl-fredonians held, that "the end, justified the means," and therefore, considered it lawful to circulate, or even to invent any lie, however gross, in order to put down their political opponents, or to promote the interest of a favourite bawler. It would be an end-less task to recount one in a thousand of the bare-faced falsehoods that were invented and circulated by the Ahramanites, for the purpose of advancing their friends to office. Should I attempt it, I might risk my reputation with posterity for veracity, as few men would believe that there ever was a race of mortals so credulous as to be oppressed and gulled for years by the most clumsy system of slander and falsehood, whilst the country contained many thousands of valiant, honourable and enlightened patriots, both willing and able to detect the fraud of their oppressors.

I shall, however, as an evidence of the *bold stroke* which these Ahramanites *played for power*, relate some of the falsehoods which were most successfully circulated, and I am the more induced to this, as I understand that in many parts of the commonwealth, there are persons yet living, who, from hearing those falsehoods so often repeated, have long mistaken them for truths.

Amongst the edicts of king John, there was one which repealed the old Hindostan law on the subject of libels, and allowing every man to write and publish what he pleased, provided it was the truth; inflicted suitable punishment upon such as should knowingly and wilfully publish any false and malicious slanders against the king or his council. No sooner was this law published, than the whole sect of Ahramanites were in an uproar. A great council was held, at which it was determined that every Ahramanite should forthwith cause it to be proclaimed in every beer-house and grog-shop throughout the kingdom, that king John and his council had resolved to establish an arbitrary government, and for this purpose had invaded the rights of the subjects, and abridged the freedom of speech. The edict was every where denounced as most tyrannical, and by common consent received the title of the gag law.— Every dishonest and ambitious wretch who wished to obtain power at the expense of a worthy competitor. Every babbling sot, who loved the grog-shop better than his farm or his work shop, and every fool, who prefered bawling to truth or reason, joined in the clamour. It was in vain that the Unionists appealed to the edict, to shew that it only prohibited wilful, false and malicious lying. Few of the Simpletonians, and none of the bawlers would give themselves the trouble of looking into the edict.*

About the same time, some Hindostanese sailors having murdered their captain on the coast of Bawlfredonia, sold the vessel and cargo. One of the pirates called Nathan Rash, when arrested, denied his country, his name and his crime, asserting that he was a native of Fredonia, from Onionville,

---

* Here it may be proper to observe, that when this edict expired, Bawlfredonius was on the throne, and his minions in the council. The Unionists asked for its revival, in order to protect them in speaking and writing the truth, respecting their rulers, but this was refused to them; the Aramanites prefered the Hindostan law, and many of the Unionists, especially in the district of Asylumonia, were severely punished for publishing some disagreeable truths respecting the Grand Lama of the Ahramanites, which they were able to prove by the most respectable testimony. But the judges who had so lately and so loudly bawled in favour of the liberty of speech, refused to hear the testimony.—*Thwackius.*

X

near Asylum harbour, where his parents still resided, and that he had no concern in the murder and piracy. However, his name, nativity, and the crime being fully proved, the offender was given up to his countrymen by order of a respectable Unionist, who held the office of Judge of the district. The law of nature and the law of God, as well as the Hindostan law, says, that "He who sheddeth man's blood, by man shall his blood be shed." Of course the murderer got the halter, with the approbation of all honest men. The Ahramanites however hold, that murder cannot be legally punished by death; and say, it is unlawful to take away the life of any, except their political opponents. They also thought the present a good opportunity to raise a clamour against king John and the Unionists, and to fix upon them the charge of partiality for the Hindostanese. The Ahramanites therefore boldly and impudently asserted, that the pirate who had met with his just deserts, was neither a murderer nor a Hindostian, but a virtuous and deserving native of Onionville, in the district of Asylum harbour, who had been kidnapped when fishing for whales on the coast, and that he had been guilty of no other offence than that of escaping from those who attempted to enslave him.

Lofty odes were addressed, "to the memory of

the gallant tar who was sacrificed to his oppressors by the wicked Unionists." Mock funerals and solemn processions were exhibited throughout Black-moreland, in honour of Nathan Robkins. Forged letters were every where handed about, purporting to have been written by the disconsolate parents of the murdered Fredonian. The libertines, who were always disposed to believe any slander against their political opponents, generally gave credit to the story, and joined in execrating the conduct of the judge, and the party to which he belonged. It was in vain that the Unionists appealed to the most respecta-ble testimony to prove that Rash was a native of Hin-dostan, a pirate and a murderer. It was equally in vain that the magistrates and ministers of the gospel, of Onionville, published their certificates, that upon the most careful search amongst their records for a century back, they could not find any account of a family or person of the name of Robkins; and the oldest and most respectable inhabitants of the village, and the principal fishermen of the district, made oath, that they never knew a person of that name in the commonwealth, and that they had never heard of any of their fishermen being kidnapped. Still the false-hood was most industriously circulated and until the present day, there are many honest folks amongst the libertines, who do actually believe, that the town of

Onionville, produced a gallant tar of the name of Nathan Robkins, that the Hindostanese kidnapped him. That after he had rescued himself by his bravery, his own countrymen, instead of protecting him, or avenging his wrongs, basely gave him up to be murdered by those who had before deprived him of his liberty!!!

FINIS.